THE PLAGUE LANDS

SUMMONED TO ANOTHER WORLD AND FORCED TO FIGHT THE DEMON KING
BOOK FOUR

JAMES E. WISHER

SAND HILL PUBLISHING

Edited by: Janie Linn Dullard

Cover art by: B-Ro

PROLOGUE

I n a dark place between realities, two beings of limitless power sat facing each other. Usually there would be nine, but today seven of the demon lords were absent. Null, the Reaper, would've happily ignored the request for a meeting, but he was curious about what the whore Ardent Lilly wanted. Though given the arrogant way she was strutting around the space, he had a strong suspicion. She was pleased about something and he could only think of one game where she was far in the lead at the moment.

Null turned his cowl to face her. As always, Ardent Lilly wore the form of a beautiful naked woman. Her dark hair seemed to shine with an inner light and her bloodred eyes glowed especially bright.

"Well?" he said. "You asked for this meeting. Say your piece."

"You're never any fun." Ardent Lilly pouted. "Given how your Chosen on Earth 73 has crushed every challenger so far, I would've thought you'd be in a better mood."

Null said nothing. His Chosen had indeed performed well

so far, but the battles never ended and neither did the great game.

"Fine. I want to know your intentions toward the hero of Valindor."

"My intentions? What makes you think I have any?"

"He's from Earth 73 and I know you've been keeping an eye on him. Any interference will result in the game ending."

"Any direct interference," Null said. "You've already pushed the boundaries of the rules by resurrecting your demon king. I doubt the others will care if I decide to push back. The game can only be ended if a majority agree and you can convince Adonael to surrender, a possibility I consider dim."

Ardent Lilly's perfect face twisted as she scowled. Somehow she even made that look beautiful. "I'll make you a side deal. Leave the hero to his own devices and when my demon king rules Valindor, I won't launch an invasion of Earth 73."

Null considered for a moment. He wanted to punish Valindor for daring to invade his Earth, and letting them suffer under Ardent Lilly's rule would certainly be a sort of punishment, albeit an unsatisfying one. As for avoiding an invasion, he doubted she'd keep her word even if she gave it. Demon lords weren't known for their honesty and she'd never submit to the sort of binding necessary to make it a guarantee.

Most importantly, if she was making the offer, she couldn't be very confident of her demon king's chances of success.

He would roll the dice.

"I decline. This hero seems strong. I'll wager on his

success. I will not directly interfere in the matter. Let the mortals fight it out as we always do."

She hissed and bared her fangs at him. "You will regret this. I swear, once Valindor is mine, I will send an army of such size Earth 73 will be reduced to a lifeless husk."

"We shall see." With that, Null vanished back to Black City. It seemed matters on Valindor were about to become a good deal more interesting. He could hardly wait to see what happened.

CHAPTER 1

Danny paused just outside the border of Fell Forest and grimaced as the aura of corruption washed over him. It had thinned out a bit since his last visit with Lyra. Closing the hell portals that had powered the dome of corruption enclosing Villipan City no doubt helped. Nevertheless, the place still turned his stomach.

Speaking of places that turned his stomach, he spun around for one last look at the Five Kingdoms. He had few good memories of his time here, but Danny liked to think he'd left the people better off than when he'd arrived. With a shake of his head, he turned back and strode down the Western Trade Road, eager to put both the land and his time as its hero behind him.

The fall weather already held a chill, but the shadows of Fell Forest made it feel even colder. He pulled his cloak tighter around him. He could use his magic to heat the air, but it wasn't that cold yet. Besides, a fair chunk of the chill was in his head rather than the atmosphere. Corruption had that effect. Once he finished the three-day journey through the forest it should get better.

Should being the operative word.

Hour after hour he hiked through the dappled shadows. No matter how high the sun rose, it never got any brighter. He was going to have three days of twilight. Luckily for Danny, he'd never been afraid of the dark.

He didn't bother stopping for lunch and eventually it began to grow properly dark. He'd have to make camp soon.

As if summoned by the thought, a faint whiff of woodsmoke tickled his nose. He paused, listening. The forest was silent as always. Monsters and demons had no use for a campfire. That meant a person had built it. Who the hell would risk traveling through Fell Forest so soon after the demon king's defeat?

Danny smiled. Other than him, of course.

His hand went to his sword hilt and he crept forward. Through the trees, a flickering orange glow appeared. Danny crouched, moving silently toward the light. He spotted the source a moment later, a small campfire, a lone figure huddled next to it. He scanned the surrounding shadows with both his mundane and magical senses and found nothing. Any enemies in the vicinity would've noticed the smoke from miles away, which meant the area was secure, for the moment at least.

Danny rose and approached, keeping his hands well away from his sword. Ten strides out it became clear the mystery camper was a woman. She sat, arms wrapped around her knees, staring into the flames. If she heard his approach, she gave no sign.

Not wanting to frighten the woman, Danny stopped and said, "Good evening."

The woman's head jerked up, eyes wide as she stared at him.

Danny held his hands out to the side to show he meant no harm. "I caught a whiff of your fire and thought I'd see who else was crazy enough to be traveling through Fell Forest."

The woman watched with seeming indifference. She should've been tense, ready to run, but after her initial reaction he saw nothing but dull lifelessness in her.

He waited for a response but after a minute it became clear he wasn't going to get one. "Would it be okay if I approached? I don't want to intrude, but when you're traveling alone it can be nice to have some company by the fire."

Finally, she gave a nearly imperceptible nod. Danny moved closer to the warmth and light. "I'm Ronin, a traveling adventurer."

She was staring at him more intently now, a hint of life in her eyes. "My name is Lise. You saved my life."

Danny frowned. He saved a lot of people during his time in the Five Kingdoms. He had no memory of this woman in particular. "Forgive me, but I don't remember you."

"I'm not surprised, it's not like we spoke. I was part of a larger group being marched through Forte by a gang of demons. You and another adventurer, a woman, set us free."

"I remember now," Danny said. "We were on our way to Forte City on a job. I'm glad you all made it to safety."

The very smallest hint of a smile tugged at her weary face. "I should be saying that to you. We all thought you'd never come back from that horrible place. As soon as we reached the village you mentioned, we offered prayers to Adonael for your safe return. It seems the archangel heard us."

JAMES E. WISHER

He had serious doubts about that but appreciated the sentiment too much to say so. "Thanks. Mind if I sit?"

Lise shrugged and gestured at a spot across from her. Danny slipped off his pack, pulled his sword out of its baldric, and settled beside the fire.

"Don't know about you, but I've been walking all day and could use a bite to eat. I've got plenty if you'd like to join me."

She didn't reply so he got out his supplies. Soon sausages were frying over the fire. The smell of fennel and onion filled the air, washing away some of the nastiness of Fell Forest.

Danny studied Lise as he cooked. He'd seldom seen such a lifeless expression. Her clothes were dirty and ragged, but once upon a time they'd been decent. The war had clearly taken a toll on her. Not that she was alone in her suffering. He shuddered to think how many others were in similar circumstances.

Curiosity got the better of him and as he turned the sausages he asked, "What brings a lady like you to a place like this?"

He doubted she was going to answer but at last she heaved a great sigh and said, "Desperation. I lost everything when the demons attacked. My husband, my children, my home, all of it. I only survived because they separated us into groups and mine was sent north while the others were killed on the spot. Pure dumb luck set me in your path. If it hadn't, I would've been sacrificed the same as they were."

Danny's heart ached for her. He knew what it meant to lose everything. It was a small kindness he hadn't left any kids behind when the summoning ritual dragged him to this world.

Lise let out a short, bitter laugh. "I say it was luck. Perhaps I was cursed. To survive while they all died is no

8

kindness. Anyway, once I'd regained my strength, I set out for the Western Trade Road. I had nothing, no plan, no hope, nothing. I just knew if I stayed in the Five Kingdoms I'd go mad from the memories. Whether I made it somewhere safe to start over or died on the way, it didn't matter. All I cared about was being somewhere else."

Danny took out a spare fork, speared one of the sausages, and held it out to her.

"Thanks." She accepted the fork and took a big bite of sausage. "It's very good."

Danny nodded. "Food always tastes better when you have someone to share it with."

They ate in silence and when they finished Lise sighed.

"Which were you hoping to find?" Danny asked. "Death or a new life?"

She stared at him, clearly taken aback by the question. Maybe he shouldn't have been so blunt, but he had to know what she wanted if he was going to help her.

And Danny had already made up his mind to help her. Given all she'd suffered, he felt a need to do something. There was no reason for it. He didn't know her; she wasn't his friend or family member. But when he saw her pain, he knew he had to do something for her.

"I honestly don't care which I find," Lise said. "I only want the pain to end. What of it?"

"If you truly want to start over, I'll escort you to the nearest village beyond Fell Forest. It's on my way and I'd appreciate the company. If not, I'll be on my way in the morning. Fell Forest will no doubt grant your other wish before long."

"You've already saved me once. You owe me nothing."

"I know that. Like I said, it's on my way. And... I'd like to help if I can. I saw a lot of death and destruction during the war. So many lives were destroyed. If I can help one person rebuild, I'd like to. So, what do you want? Deep down, what do you want?"

She gazed into the fire, fresh tears glimmering. "I want to live."

He barely heard the words, but even so he made out the iron in them. She was strong, no doubt about that.

"Good. Get some rest. We've a long journey ahead of us."

Lise nodded and looked at him across the fire. "Thank you, Ronin, for everything."

Danny smiled. "You're very welcome, Lise. See you in the morning."

As she stretched out on the ground, Danny spread out his bedroll. It took only a moment to set a ward around their camp. Fell Forest might seem empty but he didn't trust it for a moment and now he had another life depending on him.

Whether that would turn out to be a good decision or not remained to be seen, but he wouldn't regret it regardless.

CHAPTER 2

Danny sat bolt upright, all signs of sleep washed away in an instant. The only thing that would cause such a reaction was the activation of his ward. He opened himself to the ether and confirmed that something had triggered the spell. Checking the area with his magical senses, he found no lingering threats. Whatever had gotten too close had already paid the price.

He pulled his boots on and climbed to his feet. The pre-dawn stillness held an eerie kind of quiet. Fell Forest was always like that. It was the lack of ordinary animals. No birds chirped and no squirrels barked from the branches. Only predators called this forest home.

Collecting his sword, Danny strode toward the edge of the ward. He'd set it big enough to make sure Lise wouldn't trigger it if she had to visit the bushes during the night.

His nostrils flared when the stink of charred flesh reached him. With an effort of will he summoned a globe of shimmering light that hovered above his head. Its glow revealed the blackened corpses of two massive crimson ogres just beyond the boundary of his ward.

Despite their size, the ogres were among the weakest enemies calling the forest home. You didn't even need magic to kill them, just skill and good steel.

Still, he was glad he'd taken the time to add a lethal component to his usual protections. Until he and Lise parted company, he'd continue to add it.

Turning his back on the grim scene, Danny walked toward the remnants of last night's campfire. He knelt, gathering a handful of dry twigs and leaves. A small incantation coaxed a flame from the kindling, and soon a fire crackled before him. The warmth did little to dispel the chill that clung to his bones—not from the morning air, but from the constant vigilance that Fell Forest demanded.

Danny placed a skillet over the flames and soon bacon was sizzling and popping merrily away. The savory scent filled the campsite, pushing some of the gloom away. No matter the world, nothing beat starting the morning with bacon.

A little ways away, Lise stirred, her eyes fluttering open as she groaned awake. Her gaze drifted across the campsite before landing on the charred remains of the ogres just beyond the ward's perimeter.

She let out a squeak of surprise. "What…"

"Relax," Danny said without looking up from the skillet. His hands were steady as he flipped the slices of meat. "The ward did its job. Hungry?"

Lise's throat worked as she swallowed and drew her knees up, wrapping her arms around them as she watched Danny cook. "I've never seen magic like that."

"Have you seen much magic?"

She let out a slightly nervous chuckle. "No, not many wizards or arcane knights visited our little village. We did have a priest of the Goddess, but his magic was nothing outstanding."

Danny took the bacon out and poured some thick cornmeal batter in. The griddle cakes fried up quickly and he handed half the food to Lise before digging in himself. They ate in relative silence, only the crackle of the fire punctuating the stillness of the forest. It was almost peaceful, at least as peaceful as Fell Forest ever got.

"Before the demon king," Lise began out of nowhere, her voice barely above the sound of the fire, "we were a regular family. My husband, my daughter…"

She trailed off, her gaze distant. Danny said nothing. He was happy to listen, but pushing her would be a mistake.

"We had a farm. It was small, but it was ours. The life of a freeholder isn't easy, but we were generally happy. We didn't even know the demon king had returned until the monsters showed up. They destroyed everything. Killed anyone that fought and took the rest prisoner. It was a nightmare." Her fingers clenched in the fabric of her tunic, knuckles whitening. "I want— I need to do more than just survive."

"Surviving's the first step," Danny said. "Eventually you'll find a new purpose. It'll take time, but the pain does fade."

A glimmer of life sparked in Lise's eyes and she offered what might have been the first smile he'd seen on her. It brightened her rather plain features and made her almost pretty.

"How does someone so young sound so wise?"

"Sounding wise is easy, being wise is harder. If you're

done, we should get moving. We've got at least two more days to the edge of Fell Forest and I'm eager to put this place behind us."

"I second that," she said, new steel in her voice.

Leaving their camp behind, Danny set out down the Western Trade Road at what he hoped would be a comfortable pace for Lise. At a minimum, she didn't complain and her breathing was steady. If she lived on a farm, she was no doubt in good shape.

"Thank you." Lise's voice had a different tone, one he hadn't heard before. "For everything. You've given me more than just protection, Ronin. You've given me a chance to... to find purpose again."

Danny grinned. It was good to see her showing a bit of spirit. He had sufficient experience with loss to understand it was only a start and that she'd have plenty of bad days ahead of her, but it was a step in the right direction.

"Glad to help. I—" He froze. A source of corruption was headed right toward them.

"What is it?" Lise asked when she noticed he'd stopped.

"Trouble. Get behind me." He drew his sword and conjured a holy ward around her. It wasn't as strong as the ones Eve made, but it should hold as long as they didn't encounter anything too strong.

Next he charged his weapon with the same energy and drew ether into his body, enhancing his strength and speed.

The source of corruption was getting closer by the moment.

He homed in on it and raised his sword to the ready position.

"Don't move, no matter what happens. I can't fight and worry about you too."

Lise nodded, her whole body tense and her hands clenched into fists. Putting her out of his mind, Danny readied himself for battle.

With a guttural roar, two of the lamprey-headed demons that had been an endless thorn in his side since the first battle he fought on this world came snarling out of the depths of Fell Forest.

Danny's grip tightened around the sword's hilt.

The first demon leapt at him.

He spun and slashed, cutting a deep groove in its side. His back cut drove the second demon back long enough for him to finish off the first one with a slash to the neck that sent its head tumbling to the dirt.

Undeterred by its companion's death, the surviving demon lunged with a high-pitched screech that hurt Danny's ears. That was a new trick, but not an effective one. Ignoring the noise, he cut the demon in half from right shoulder to left hip.

Both bodies immediately started dissolving into black goo.

As soon as he confirmed the area was clear he released all his spells. As fights went, it was far from the hardest he'd fought since arriving on Valindor, but without the hero's armor or his ethersword, it made for a bit of a challenge.

He sheathed his sword and turned to Lise. "We're good. You okay?"

The tremors in Lise's hands made it clear she was far from okay. She hurried over and clung to Danny, her fingers digging into his dark tunic as she hugged him.

"Those were the same ones that attacked our village. I thought... I thought..."

She didn't seem capable of finishing the sentence. Danny

well understood the triggers of PTSD. He just hugged her and waited until the trembling stopped.

"If you're up to it, we need to get going."

"Right." She backed away and looked up at him. "I'm okay now."

He let the lie pass and they continued on, the road stretching endlessly before them. Thankfully the rest of the day and the next night passed without incident. Around midafternoon the next day, Fell Forest opened up, revealing an expanse of fields and rolling hills.

They'd made it through.

Unfortunately, there wasn't a sign of civilization to be found as far as he could see. That wasn't a surprise since no one in their right mind would build close to Fell Forest.

"What now?" Lise asked. "I wasn't sure we'd make it through the forest and now that we have, it doesn't feel real."

"Oh, it's real. I figure if we stick to the road we'll reach a village eventually. Once we do, you can start your new life. As for me, my destination is still a long ways from here."

"Maybe you could settle down instead." She looked up at him, seeming a bit nervous.

Danny swallowed a sigh. He was afraid of this. Even though he'd tried his best not to encourage her, it looked like Lise had gotten attached to him. While he would never regret helping her, this was a complication he didn't need.

"No, my mission can't be set aside. Too much is on the line. You're a strong, capable woman. I'm sure you'll find your place in no time."

She sniffed and wiped her eyes. "Right. We're practically strangers after all. Not to mention I'm old enough to be your mother. Forget I said anything."

Forgetting about it struck Danny as an excellent idea. "I'd

like to put some distance between us and Fell Forest before dark, assuming you're up to more walking."

"I'm good. Let's go." She set out down the road and Danny followed along behind.

Whoever ended up marrying her was going to have his hands full in the best way possible.

CHAPTER 3

Danny stopped on the crest of a low hill and shaded his eyes against the glare of the noon sun. Five days of steady walking had put Fell Forest well behind them. While he knew no one would build a village close to the corrupt forest, he never imagined they'd have to walk this far to find civilization.

Lise's stamina had proven a welcome surprise. She'd kept up without a word of complaint. Danny didn't set a blistering pace, but he'd walked right along. His best guess put them a hundred miles from the forest.

"We found something. Finally," Danny said.

The little village nestled between two hills wasn't huge by Five Kingdom standards. A rough dirt path turned off the main trade road and ran down to the village. It had a palisade fence surrounding it and a wagon served as a sort of gate. From here, despite using a spell to enhance his vision, he couldn't see a soul moving around either in the village itself or in the nearby fields.

"Looks abandoned," Lise said.

"Yup, but let's take a closer look to make sure." They turned down the path and Danny moved a little ahead of Lise. If there was trouble he wanted to reach it first.

He needn't have worried. The village was as still and silent up close as it had been at a distance. It also stank to high heaven. The wagon blocking the entrance had been turned on its side. Whoever put it there clearly didn't want anyone moving it easily. A crude white skull with an X through it had been painted on the wagon bed. The sight triggered a memory in Danny's host.

That was a plague sign.

The memory sent a shiver down Danny's spine. He cast a sideways glance at Lise, and saw her expression was twisted in disgust.

"What's that smell?" she asked.

"Rotting bodies." Danny didn't need his host to provide the answer. He'd smelled the same stench in a slaughtered village his team stumbled on during his first deployment. That was a memory he'd never forget. "You recognize the plague mark?"

She nodded but didn't speak.

"I can't imagine someone's still alive in there, but let's take a look just to be sure," Danny said.

"Going in there's a bad idea," Lise said. "I don't even like being this close to it."

"You can wait here. My magic will keep any disease at bay. I won't be long."

Lise shook her head and grabbed his arm. "I'm not staying out here alone. Whatever's waiting, I prefer to face it with you."

"Alright." He wasn't going to insist she stay behind. A village full of corpses should be safe. Assuming they were properly dead and not just waiting for some unlucky sap to show up so they could attack.

A moment of concentration surrounded him and Lise with a golden aura of Heavenly magic. Though it would stop any illness from reaching them, it did nothing to stop the smell.

A hard, magically enhanced shove moved the wagon out of the way, allowing them to enter. Danny kept the lead as they walked down the village's lone street. Lise had a death grip on his left arm, as if she thought he might disappear on her.

They approached the first house, a simple structure that couldn't have more than three rooms. Its door was partway open as if in unspoken invitation to enter.

Danny stuck his head in and grimaced. Three bodies lay on the floor in pools of fluid he preferred not to examine too closely.

He jerked his head back. "You don't want to look."

"I certainly don't," Lise agreed.

Methodically, Danny checked each dwelling, finding only bodies. Given the level of decay, he figured this place had been sealed up for a month or so. As far as he could tell, no animals had come sniffing around. That was strange. Crows at least should have been feasting.

When they'd checked the last house Danny said, "Nothing living."

As he expected, but it was no less depressing for the lack of surprise.

"Let's get the hell out of here," Lise said. "I've had enough of dead villages to last a lifetime."

Danny nodded, happy to leave the place behind.

When they'd put a hundred yards and the worst of the

smell behind them, Lise let out a long breath. "That was so much worse than what happened to my village."

He reached out and placed a hand on her shoulder. "I'm sorry, Lise. I didn't intend to bring up bad memories."

"No." She swallowed hard. "We needed to be sure. I understand that."

"Stand still." He opened himself to the ether and bathed them both in the white glow of holy energy. He was confident the barrier kept any disease at bay, but after what he saw in those houses, Danny wasn't taking any chances.

"Let's get out of here," Danny said. "Maybe we can find some living people to tell us what's going on."

"Settling around here suddenly seems a good deal less appealing than I first thought," Lise said.

Danny couldn't fault her logic.

Leaving the forsaken village, they retraced their steps back to the trade road. He had no idea how far apart villages were spaced in this part of the world, but hopefully it wouldn't take them another five days to find out.

"I'm getting sick of this road," he muttered.

"As long as it takes us somewhere alive," she said. "I don't care about anything else."

He smiled despite the grimness of their situation. Lise had a knack for cutting to the heart of the matter.

They continued on, determined to put as much distance between themselves and the plague village as the sun would allow. Tomorrow was another day. If heaven stood with them it would be a better one.

CHAPTER 4

A new village appeared on the horizon in the middle of the afternoon two days after they left the plague village behind. From a distance it looked pretty much the same as the first one: same palisade, same simple houses. The main difference was a crude gate in place of the wagon. That and the living people outside the gate.

That the four men held crossbows cradled in their arms was less encouraging. Though given what Danny had seen so far, it was hardly a surprise. At least the walk hadn't been as long as Danny feared.

"What do you think?" Lise asked as they pressed on.

"I think living guards are an upgrade from a plague-marked wagon. Hopefully they don't shoot on sight. It wouldn't do any good, but I'd still prefer to avoid violence."

"I second that."

They turned off the main road and made a beeline for the village.

Twenty yards out, the center guard shouted, "Stop where you are!"

Danny obliged, raising his hands in a gesture of peace as he did. The guards had their crossbows raised, fingers on the trigger ready to fire. That was terrible trigger discipline, but he saw no point in saying so. Judging from their ragged leathers and rusty bits of mail, these weren't the finest soldiers in the land. At least Danny hoped they weren't.

"We mean you no harm," he said.

"State your business!" the same guard said. His eyes were narrow and suspicious beneath the brim of his iron helm.

"We're travelers," Danny said, keeping his tone calm and even. "A hot meal and a bed would be most welcome if you can spare them."

"Travelers?" The guard spat the word. "What sort of fool travels when the plague is spreading?"

Danny understood the guard's fear. He couldn't do anything about it, but he understood it.

"We didn't know about the plague when we set out and we can't go back in any case." Danny shrugged. "Is there any way we can convince you to let us in? It's been far too long since we enjoyed a bit of civilization."

The guards exchanged uneasy glances, their fingers twitching above the triggers of their crossbows. They clearly had no idea what to do. Fear seldom led to good decisions, but, so far at least, they'd refrained from shooting. That had to be a good sign.

"Hang on a minute," the central guard said at last. "Len, go fetch Father Wolter. He can tell us if these two are safe."

The youngest of the guards slipped under the bar that blocked access to the village and hurried out of sight.

Minutes dragged by. Danny took some comfort in the guards lowering their weapons. It seemed they'd calmed enough to recognize Danny and Lise weren't an immediate threat.

"Do you think they're going to let us in?" Lise asked, her voice pitched low so there was no danger of the guards overhearing.

"Hopefully, once their priest confirms we're not sick. At least, I can't see any reason they'd refuse us once it's safe."

At last, the young guard reappeared, along with a skinny, middle-aged man dressed in a white robe featuring the red cross of the Goddess, Lady of Healing. Father Wolter looked them all over. Danny could feel the ether filling his eyes, though he didn't recognize the specific spell.

"They're clear," the priest said, a note of relief in his voice. "No taint of plague upon them."

The guards relaxed, shoulders slumping and crossbows dipping toward the ground. The center guard waved them closer. Up close, it was clear he'd seen plenty of years. His scruffy beard was flecked with white and a nasty scar ran down the side of his face.

"In with you then," he said, motioning them through. "We don't have a proper tavern, but I'm sure someone would be willing to sell you a meal. Mind your manners and don't cause trouble. Branik knows we've seen enough of it. Welcome to White Hall."

"Thank you and rest assured we'll be on our best behavior," Danny said.

"If you're willing," Father Wolter said. "I'll introduce you to Mayor Rik. I'm sure he'll be eager for news of the outside world."

"That works for me," Danny said. "I'd like to know more about what's happening around here before we resume our journey."

Father Wolter bowed to them and led the way into the village. As they walked down the dirt path that divided the village in half, Danny spotted nervous people peeking out at them only to pull back when he looked their way.

"Don't mind their curiosity," Father Wolter said. "We seldom had visitors before the plague. Now, a new arrival is a potential threat as well as a diversion."

Danny didn't mind in the least and resolved to ignore them.

Soon they arrived outside the largest house in the village. Not that it was anything special, just a bigger version of the standard design. Father Wolter knocked and a moment later the door opened, revealing a woman in her fifties dressed in a tan dress with a white apron over it. She looked them over, a little frown creasing her forehead.

"Is Mayor Rik available?" Father Wolter asked. "We have guests and I'm sure he'll want to speak with them."

"Of course he's available," the woman said. "The lazy lout has nothing to keep him occupied now. He sits around muttering to himself until I can't stand it and kick him out for a few hours. Then he comes back and starts all over again. Come in and I'll fetch him."

She shuffled off deeper into the house while Danny and his companions waited in the central room. There were a few chairs around a rough table. He figured it served as both a dining room and living room.

"I'm guessing that's the mayor's wife," Lise said.

"You would be correct," Father Wolter said. "If she doesn't drag him out by the ear I'll be impressed."

"Welcome, travelers." Danny started when the first fat man he'd seen in a long time entered the room. Mayor Rik wore a billowing tunic that would've been called a

25

muumuu back home. "What brings you to our cursed land?"

Father Wolter sighed. "Don't be so dramatic, Rik. Terrible though it might be, a plague isn't the same as a curse."

"We've come from the Five Kingdoms." Danny paused but the name brought no reaction. "I'm Ronin, an elite adventurer, simply passing through on my way further west while Lise is looking for a place to settle. Neither of us had any idea what to expect when we left Fell Forest behind. Then we came across a village." Danny laid out everything they found.

"We hoped Green Rock had simply hunkered down, the same as us." The mayor scrubbed a hand across his face. "Three of our own have fallen ill. We keep them isolated, but the longer the illness goes on, the greater the chance of others catching it. The power you used to purify yourselves, could you use it to cure them?"

"Your healer…" Danny turned toward Father Wolter.

"He has done all within his power," the priest cut in, his face a mask of sorrow. "But I lack the strength to defeat this disease."

"I don't know," Danny said. "But I'm willing to try."

"Heaven bless you," Father Wolter said.

"Indeed," Mayor Rik said. "Succeed or fail, we appreciate you trying. Show them the way, Wolter."

The priest led them out and across the village to an isolated house. Two masked guards armed with crossbows stood on duty outside. Both men nodded to Wolter but didn't speak.

"This gentleman will be attempting to cure the afflicted. He has my and the mayor's permission to enter."

The men shifted aside to let Danny pass.

"Be careful," Lise said.

He appreciated her concern, but this wasn't a real battle. His divine barrier would protect him from whatever virus was behind the plague. The only question was whether or not he could cure the disease with a simple application of holy energy. He knew it would accelerate the healing of wounds, but neither Danny nor his host body had any idea how the technique would work on the plague.

There was one way to find out. Steeling himself, he pushed through the door.

CHAPTER 5

Danny hadn't spent much time around really sick people. He visited his grandfather in the hospital once when he was a kid and that was about it. The antiseptic smell had been awful, but it had nothing on the scent of disease filling the isolation house. It kind of clung to the back of your throat and refused to let go. He wished his holy aura blocked that smell as well as it did the germs.

Two men lay stretched out and unmoving on narrow beds. A woman sat in a hard chair between them, her head bowed, whether in exhaustion or in prayer he couldn't say. Perhaps it was a little of both.

She looked up, her eyes hollow from watching and waiting. "Are you here to die with us?"

Danny barely heard her above the labored breathing of the men she tended.

"No, ma'am." Danny knelt beside the first patient, a young man about the same age as his host body. The man's skin was hot to the touch, his breath coming in ragged gasps. He didn't look long for the world.

He flicked a glance at the woman and found her staring at the floor again, head hanging as if she lacked the strength to look up. It was rather pitiful, but convenient. He opened his storage and pulled out the ethersword's hilt. With the mithril to enhance his magic, Danny figured he'd have the best chance of success.

Channeling ether through the hilt then out into the patient, he envisioned the pure energy flooding every cell in his body, strengthening what belonged and burning away what didn't.

Seizures shook the unlucky fellow, but Danny didn't stop. Eventually the thrashing ended and he sensed that the healing was complete. Exactly how he sensed it was another matter. It was magic after all and he had to trust that it was working the way it was supposed to.

Danny repeated the process with the second man. He wasn't quite as weak and so withstood the process easier. Finally he purified the woman and himself along with every surface in the house.

He'd barely returned the hilt to storage when the woman looked up, her eyes wide. "What was that?"

"Magic. All three of you are disease free. Father Wolter will have to confirm it, but I'm confident you're out of danger. Stay strong. You'll all need time to fully recover, but you will recover."

"Heaven bless you, sir. I thought I was going to lose them both."

"I'm glad I could help." Danny stood, wobbled, and went to the door. That had been a bit of a job and he was looking forward to a nice rest. He waved to the priest. "It's done."

Father Wolter hurried over but didn't enter. Instead he stared at them all with the same intense look he'd used at the gate. After a minute he said, "I can't believe it. There's no sign of the disease in any of you. We'll keep the others in the isolation house until morning, but if they're still disease free, I'll let them return home. You can come out."

Danny stepped into the light and took a deep breath of fresh air. His body still tingled from all the ether he'd channeled. It was a different feeling from when he used physical enhancement and he wasn't quite sure what to make of it. It wasn't painful and did keep him safe from the plague, so all in all he'd call it a small price.

When he'd put a safe distance between himself and the isolation house, Lise hurried over. "Are you okay?"

"I'm fine, thanks. More importantly, the spell worked. Looks like they're going to be okay."

"That's a relief." She moved to give him a hug, paused, and seemed to think better of it.

Danny was okay with putting a little distance between them. He was going to be parting company with Lise at some point in the not-too-distant future, so keeping her from getting any more attached was prudent.

Father Wolter headed their way. "I need to let Rik know the magic worked. He'll want to have a celebration tonight. We've had nothing but bad news for a while and this will lift the people's spirits."

Danny had no great interest in being the center of attention, but he also understood the importance of morale. "I'm looking forward to it. For now, is there somewhere I can rest?"

"Of course," Father Wolter said. "Forgive my lack of consideration. It isn't much, but you're welcome to use my home for as long as you need. This way."

They followed the priest to the far side of the village

where his modest home waited. It had a little altar dedicated to the Goddess in the central room, a small kitchen and an equally small bedroom. The village's lone priest wasn't living in luxury by any means. It raised Danny's already good opinion of Wolter a couple more notches.

"Rest here as long as you like." Wolter offered a little bow before hurrying away.

Danny yawned. It would be weird sleeping in the man's bed, so he spread his bedroll out on the floor and lay down. An effort of will set a non-lethal ward around the room. Danny doubted they were in any danger here, but he'd been attacked so many times he didn't want to risk it.

"What are we going to do?" Lise asked. "Long term. With the plague going around, I don't think settling in the area is going to work. People are too afraid of strangers."

"Though it's going to delay my mission," Danny said. "A lot of people are going to die if someone doesn't figure out what's causing this plague. At a minimum, tracking down its origin and learning how it's spreading would give them a fighting chance even if there isn't a cure."

"It doesn't have to be you who does it," Lise said.

"True, but with my magic I'm basically immune. That makes me the best person for the job. Don't misunderstand, I'm not making any firm plans until I know more and I'll be sure to find a safe place for you first. Protecting only myself takes a lot less power than protecting both of us."

Lise chewed her lip but didn't ask any more questions. Danny was grateful for her consideration and closed his eyes to rest.

His rest lasted for a few hours before the sound of many voices laughing and shouting got his attention. He sat up and yawned. The tingling was gone and all his parts were functioning properly. He didn't think he'd slept, but the rest had done him good.

Lise was seated in one of the hard chairs and had her feet up on another. The soft snores made it clear she'd had better luck getting to sleep than he did.

Not wanting to wake her, Danny tiptoed over to the door and pushed it open. Outside, a group of villagers was gathering wood for a bonfire while others were setting up tables nearby. It appeared the celebration was to be an outside one. Made sense given the size of the houses.

Judging by the length of the shadows, they still had a couple more hours until dark. He closed the door and pulled the gazetteer out of storage. He wanted to confirm a few things. Given their rough location he still had at least fifteen hundred miles to go to reach Elfhome. All the measurements were rough so he couldn't say for sure. Even if he found a safe place for Lise, traveling through this plague-cursed land was going to slow him down.

Worse than that, winter would soon be here in earnest. Danny wasn't sure what the seasons were like in this part of the world, but given the unchanging latitude he was traveling along, it should be similar to the Five Kingdoms. Based on his host's memories that meant about six weeks of really cold weather starting in a month or so followed by a nasty, wet couple of months that passed as spring. Not exactly great traveling weather.

There were two cities between here and Elfhome. Hopefully they were still there and thriving.

His research continued until three heavy blows on the door startled him out of his planning. Danny quickly put his book away before Lise could fully wake up. As she rubbed her eyes, he opened the door.

Father Wolter was outside. Behind him dusk had fallen and the bonfire was blazing. Looked like the entire village was there.

"Party time?" Danny asked.

"Indeed. Rik wants to make a quick thank-you speech, then we'll eat."

"Eating sounds good." Lise came over to join them.

"Then come along," Father Wolter said. "Our food is simple, but I hope you'll enjoy it."

They made the short walk to the gathering. As soon as the chubby mayor spotted them he waved from his place at the head of the largest table. "Over here. Our guests of honor have arrived at last." His voice carried easily despite the many chattering voices.

The villagers went silent and Danny tensed a bit when their eyes focused on him. The reactions were mixed, some still tinged with disbelief, others carrying a hint of reverence. The latter made him more nervous than the former.

"Your magic is a great gift," Mayor Rik said, his tone somber. "We feared the Nulen clan had no hope of survival, but thanks to this brave adventurer, Ronin, they've been cured of the plague."

A huge roar went up from the gathered villagers.

"And so, in celebration of this miracle, we feast and give thanks for this life Heaven has granted us. Huzzah!"

"Huzzah!" the villagers shouted in response.

Danny had never heard that cheer before but it sounded heartfelt. He also appreciated the brevity of the mayor's speech. Everyone settled at a table and Danny ended up between the mayor and Lise with Wolter across from him, which was perfect as far as he was concerned.

Dishes were soon brought out from various houses, most

of them consisting of braised meat and root vegetables. There were also great quantities of beer, an especially bitter variety that Danny had trouble choking down.

When they'd eaten a few bites the mayor said, "We can never thank you enough, though I fear when you leave we will once more be in danger of the plague returning."

It wasn't the subtlest of hints, but since Danny had already decided to look into the matter he was happy to play along. "Do you know where it came from?"

"None. We're pretty isolated here. Sometimes our shepherds meet shepherds from Green Rock or one of the other nearby villages. The fields are open to everyone and there's plenty of grass to go around. Merchants visit a few times a year. And of course we trade with the beastfolk hunters. My best guess is young Rem Nulen ran into a sick shepherd from Green Rock and brought it back with him. If he's awake, I mean to ask him in the morning."

"I'd like to join you," Danny said. "Where would I go from here if I wanted to find out what was going on in the greater area?"

"Redfield, to the northwest, is the biggest town in the area. All the merchants go there. As for speaking with Rem, you're more than welcome to join in. If anyone's earned the right, you have. And thank you for looking into the disease. No one here is up to it, but with your magic, maybe you can find a way to end the plague."

"I'll do my best." Danny just hoped his best would be good enough.

CHAPTER 6

Danny had drunk some nasty coffee during his time as a Marine, but right now he would've happily sipped the worst of it rather than the mug of heated beer Father Wolter had provided him this morning. He didn't know how the stuff could be worse hot, but it was. Lise, seated opposite him at the dining room table in Father Wolter's modest home, sipped hers without making a face. He couldn't have been more impressed.

Their host emerged from the kitchen carrying three bowls of coarse grits cooked with sheep's milk. He set one in front of each of his guests before sitting himself.

"Mayor Rik won't be up early, especially after last night," Father Wolter said.

Danny took a bite of his grits and found them a thousand times better than the beer. They had a smooth texture and hint of sweetness he quite liked. "I'm not in a huge rush. A little extra rest wouldn't hurt my feelings after all the walking we've done."

"Agreed," Lise said.

They ate in companionable silence. When the last of the grits were gone Danny asked, "Have you visited Redfield?"

"I did my training there," Father Wolter said. "Four years at the Goddess's temple. Those were happy times despite my limited ability. Redfield is a lively place. It serves as a base for all the merchants in the area. Each of the archangels has a temple. There's even an adventurer's guild."

Danny grinned. That was exactly what he'd been hoping to hear. "Sounds like a good place to track down some leads."

"Why are some priests stronger than others?" Lise asked. "I don't know much about it, but I thought you were channeling the archangel's power. Shouldn't it be the same for everyone?"

"The Goddess's power is the same for everyone. The problem is, not everyone is equally compatible with the ether which she uses as a medium to deliver it to us. Like wizards, some priests are stronger than others. That's just the way it is."

"Doesn't seem fair," Lise said. "Not that much else does."

Danny hated the bitterness in her voice, but he couldn't argue with the truth of her words. He was well aware of the world's unfairness.

About an hour later someone knocked and Mayor Rik's voice came through the door. "Are you ready, Ronin?"

Danny hopped to his feet and crossed the room. He opened the door and found the mayor's rotund figure waiting outside. "I am. Lead the way."

"Come along, Wolter," Mayor Rik said. "We need you to confirm they haven't relapsed."

"I'm coming, I'm coming." Wolter crossed the room and stepped out into the street.

Danny turned back to Lise. "We shouldn't be long. Do you mind waiting here?"

"I'll be fine. Go do what you have to. I assume we'll be leaving as soon as you get back."

Danny nodded. "That's my plan. We've got plenty of daylight left."

Lise gave him a little goodbye wave and the three men set out across the village. It was every bit as quiet as when Danny arrived.

When he mentioned it, Mayor Rik said, "The shepherds have already gone out to relieve the night watch. Everyone else is no doubt working inside. Not much happens day in and day out around here."

Considering everything that had happened since he got here, Danny didn't think that was such a bad thing.

They reached the isolation house and found two new guards on duty, their masks firmly in place.

One of the guards nodded as they approached, his eyes weary above the cloth covering his mouth and nose. "Mayor. How much longer will we have to keep watch?"

"Assuming the Nulens are still healthy, you can return to your regular duties as soon as we leave," Mayor Rik said.

"That'd be a relief, sir." The guard knocked twice.

A moment later the woman answered, her face still pale but better than yesterday.

"Morning, Lottie," Mayor Rik said. "How are you all doing?"

"Much better." Lottie turned a fraction to focus on Danny. "Thank you for yesterday. The words seem inadequate but they're all I have to offer."

"Your words and recovery are all the reward I need," Danny said.

"Is Rem up?" Mayor Rik asked. "We need to talk to him."

"He's awake but resting. Come in, please." She stepped aside to let them enter.

The mayor looked to Father Wolter, who nodded. "I sense no disease anywhere in the house. It's safe."

Danny followed the mayor and Father Wolter into the dimly lit room where Rem lay in his bed. He was sitting up today with the help of several pillows. The young man turned toward them and offered a weak smile. In the bed beside him his father snored away, blissfully unaware of his visitors.

"Rem, how do you feel, my boy?" Mayor Rik asked.

"Better, sir, thank you," Rem said, his voice weak. "Much better than before. Is this the adventurer who saved me?"

"That's right. Rem, this is Ronin. It was only by heaven's grace that he happened to arrive in time to heal you all."

"Much obliged, sir," Rem said.

Danny grinned. "My pleasure, Rem. As a rule, I much prefer saving lives to taking them."

"We had a couple questions if you're up to it," Mayor Rik said.

"Yes, sir. I'm okay."

"Before you got sick, did you meet any outsiders? A shepherd from Green Rock maybe?"

"No, sir. I haven't seen anyone from Green Rock in a month. They're grazing more east and north, hoping to get the last of the clover before it freezes. The only person I've met from outside is Alder, he's one of the beastfolk hunters we trade with regular. He passed by my flock on the trail of an Alpha Wolf. I didn't see any tracks so he was probably on its scent. He paused to warn me and we shared a drink of beer. You know how they like it."

"That I do," Mayor Rik said. "Did Alder seem... okay?"

Rem cocked his head then his eyes widened. "He wasn't sick, sir, if that's what you mean. I never seen a sick beastfolk and Alder seemed strong as an ox. If he was sick then I don't know what sick is."

"Do you still have the skin you shared?" Danny asked.

"Sure, it's back home. Why?"

Danny shook his head. "Just curious. You should rest. It'll take some time for your strength to return, so don't push yourself."

"I won't," Rem said. "And thank you again for saving me."

Danny held out his hand and Rem gave it a weak shake. "You're very welcome. Take care."

No one had any other questions so the trio took their leave. As soon as they were outside the mayor dismissed the men on guard duty.

"Well, that didn't amount to much," Rik said.

"Not necessarily. Where's Rem's house? I'd like Father Wolter to take a look at that skin."

"Why?" Father Wolter asked.

"In case the plague lingered. It may not have given how much time has passed, but I'd like to make sure."

"Rem said the beastfolk wasn't sick."

"Some people can carry a disease and never get sick themselves," Danny said. "It's possible this hunter was immune and didn't know he was a carrier."

Mayor Rik's brow furrowed. "The Nulens live a few houses from here. Come on."

A few strides later Mayor Rik asked, "How could someone have the disease and not get sick?"

Danny shook his head. "I have no idea how it works. Everyone reacts to an illness differently. And I might be completely wrong. No one can say for sure without having a priest examine the hunter in question."

"We're already checking everyone that approaches the town," Father Wolter said. "We'll have to warn the shepherds not to let anyone get close when they're outside the wall. That will be difficult for them, but given the alternative…"

They all knew what the alternative meant.

"This is it." Mayor Rik stopped in front of a house that looked just like all the others.

"I'll go in alone," Danny said. "If I find the skin, Father Wolter can check it from a safe distance."

Danny pushed through the open door and into the cluttered space beyond. Cloaks hung on hooks by the door, the dining area was neat and the table set for three. In the kitchen Danny spotted a leather drinking skin on the counter. That had to be it. He grabbed it and headed back to the door.

"One moment." Father Wolter gave the skin the familiar, intent look. "It's very faint, but I can see a hint of plague at the spout. It could just as well have come from Rem as the hunter."

"True," Danny said. "I'll purify the whole house just to be safe."

He focused and sent a mist of ether charged with holy energy throughout the house like a spray from a disinfectant. That done, he hung the flask by the cloaks and stepped outside.

"I think I've done about all I can here. Hopefully I can learn more in Redfield. I wish you the best of luck."

"Same to you, my friend," Rik said.

"Indeed, may the Goddess watch over you," Father Wolter added.

Danny didn't know what sort of standing he had in Heaven at the moment, but he'd take all the help he could get.

CHAPTER 7

The town of Redfield was built directly on the Western Trade Road. A thirty-foot-tall heavy wooden wall topped with spikes surrounded it and even from a distance Danny could see the noon sun glinting off the helmets of guards patrolling the battlements. It had taken nearly a week for Danny and Lise to make the walk from White Hall. Which was less time than Mayor Rik warned them they'd need. The fact that they weren't herding sheep no doubt sped their journey a fair bit.

The sheer peacefulness of the walk had surprised Danny, though in retrospect it shouldn't have. No one who didn't have to would be traveling when a plague was spreading. They had seen a small group of beastfolk, at least Danny assumed they were given the pointed ears sticking up from their heads, but as soon as he looked their way they took off. Shy was better than aggressive, but he would've liked to chat with them.

"Doesn't look like we'll be getting in any time soon," Lise said.

Danny grimaced at the line of wagons waiting to enter Redfield. There had to be over a dozen ahead of them, and the line was moving at an agonizing crawl. He swallowed a sigh. Despite his time in the military, patience was not a virtue he'd acquired.

"No, it doesn't. But hopefully it won't take too long. A proper meal would suit me well."

"Do you think we can get a bath?" Lise's desperation brought a smile to Danny's face. "I haven't had a proper bath in months."

"Hopefully. Though I have no idea what services the inns in this town offer."

"Any news from Little Creek?" the merchant ahead of them asked his traveling companion. He kept his voice so low that Danny barely heard him.

"Not in weeks. The three villages I visited before meeting up with you seemed okay, but they hadn't heard anything either. What about Green Rock?"

The first man shook his head. "I passed by but the mayor warned me away. Half the village was sick and he didn't sound optimistic. Damned plague. Where do you think it came from? There hasn't been a serious outbreak since Red Fever swept through the valley in my great-grandfather's time."

"Heaven knows. People survived the fever and people will survive whatever this is. It's our bad luck it happened during our lifetimes."

Danny walked around the side of the wagon, careful not to get too close. "Beg your pardon, but I couldn't help over-hearing. Do you know how far the plague has spread?"

The passenger, a rugged-looking fellow in his midtwenties, laid a hand on the stock of his crossbow and glared at Danny. "What business is it of yours?"

"It's everyone's business," Danny said. "I passed by Green Rock on my way here. Not a soul survived. White Hall was better. Mayor Rik told me to come to Redfield if I was looking for work. I'm Ronin, elite adventurer."

"You're sure everyone was dead?" the driver asked.

"Yes. It was horrible."

The driver shook his head. "I wish I was less surprised. Little Creek likely suffered the same fate. I know Rik. It's good to hear his town is holding its own. I'm glad this was my last trip until spring, I can tell you that. I wish I had more details to share, but most of the towns I visited knew nothing about it. I passed a warning along, but that's all I could do."

"I'm not from this area," Danny said. "Is there no central authority that can help with the situation?"

The younger man barked a laugh. "There's no authority here. The villages handle their own business, the temples help out where they can, and the guilds take as much of the profits as possible."

"And that's the way we like it," the older man added. "Usually, at least. Where might you be from, sir?"

"The Five Kingdoms, are you familiar with it?"

"I've heard of it, but never risked the trip through the cursed woods to trade there."

"Fell Forest is definitely not to be traversed lightly. My companion and I made it through with little trouble, but a larger group might attract more attention. I appreciate you taking the time to chat with me."

"Not at all, sir." The driver gave him a nod and urged his wagon ahead a few yards.

"They seemed reasonably friendly," Lise said when Danny had rejoined her. "Though the news could've been better."

"True. Of course, given everything we've seen, the bad news was hardly a shock."

"Do these people truly have no lord to watch over them?"

"Sounds that way. Not sure if that's better or worse, but it's certainly different from the Five Kingdoms."

After a tedious hour of inching forward a wagon length at a time, they finally reached the gate. A squad of city guards flanked the entrance, spears glinting in the sun. Their faces were obscured by cloth masks. Word of the plague had clearly reached Redfield. Danny had serious doubts about the usefulness of those masks given the lack of magic in them, but maybe they made the guards feel better.

A grim, scowling priest in dark robes stood behind the wall of spearmen. He wore a chain hoop around his neck, marking him as a follower of the Binder. Of all the faiths they might've encountered, his was the one Danny most wanted to avoid. Mostly because of their reputation. Eve hadn't made them sound pleasant. Not that her patron, Adonael, was on Danny's Christmas card list either.

The guards poked and prodded merchants' wares with the blunt ends of their spears, looking for all the world like they expected someone to leap up and make a run for it. The priest stared at the men with the same intense look Father Wolter used to root out plague bearers.

After a tense few minutes the priest said, "They're free of disease."

One of the guards approached the driver. "Two gold coins."

"Two!" the driver said. "Three months ago it was five silvers."

"Three months ago there wasn't a plague requiring the constant employment of a priest at the gate. Pay or leave, it's your choice."

Grumbling about banditry, the merchant handed over the coins and urged his wagon through.

"Next!" the lead guard said.

Danny and Lise stepped forward.

"You're not merchants," the guard said. "What's your business in Redfield?"

"I'm an adventurer on my way further west. I'm just passing through. I ran into Lise on the way and we've been traveling together. Thought this would be a good place to rest for a few days and buy supplies. Would you like to see my badge?"

The guard looked back at the priest, who nodded. "They're free from disease."

"Hand it over." Danny dug the badge out of his satchel and passed it to the guard who gave it a cursory glance before handing it back. "One gold coin."

Danny handed over a small gold coin. The guard gave the Five Kingdoms' currency a funny look then bit it. Seeming satisfied, he dropped it into the pouch at his side.

"Go on."

"Thank you, sir. Good afternoon."

Danny strode through the gate to find the cobbled streets of Redfield stretching out before him. The main street was lined with businesses, including stalls selling everything you could think of. Especially food. The savory scent of roasting meat wafted from a nearby stall. It was almost enough to forget what was happening beyond the walls.

Almost.

"What do you say we grab a bite before finding an inn? I

don't know about you, but a meal that isn't jerky, bacon, or griddle cakes would suit me very well."

Lise mustered a smile. "I could eat."

They approached a stall where a heavyset man was turning spits of meat over a crackling fire. Danny inhaled the mouthwatering aroma. "Smells delicious. Two orders of whatever that is, please."

As the cook loaded rolls with fragrant cuts of meat and sliced onion, Danny leaned in. "My companion and I just arrived in town. Any suggestions on reputable inns?"

The man shot them a look as he worked. "The Golden Gate is four buildings down. They cater to strangers. Two silver coins for the food."

"Much obliged." Danny handed him three small silver coins, then passed an over-full sandwich to Lise. They found an empty spot a few feet away and fell to eating. The meat was delicious if a bit on the tough side. Danny figured it was mutton since he hadn't seen anything but sheep since he arrived in the area.

When he finally looked up from his half-eaten sandwich he found Lise staring at hers with a blank expression.

"Hey," Danny said. "Copper for your thoughts."

"I was just thinking I left one horrible situation for another one every bit as awful in its own way. Is it too much to ask for a bit of peace and quiet with no one dying or getting killed?"

"In this life? Probably."

"Wow, you're really bad at giving reassurance. You're supposed to say, 'don't worry, Lise, we'll find a place like that one day.'"

Danny allowed himself a grim smile. "If you're looking for happy lies, you're traveling with the wrong guy. What say we get ourselves settled at the Golden Gate? Hopefully they have a tub and you can soak your cares away."

"That sounds lovely." She resumed eating with some enthusiasm.

When they finished the sandwiches, Danny led the way down the street until he spotted a large, two-story building with a sign featuring a golden arch. He assumed this had to be the place and pushed through the door.

The Golden Gate Inn was slammed. Patrons jostled for space at the bar while harried servers wove through the crowd balancing trays laden with foaming tankards and steaming bowls. This was clearly the place to go for lunch. Danny cut a path through the chaos, one hand on Lise's elbow as he steered them toward the back of the room.

"Stay close," he murmured, pitching his voice low enough that no one would hear over the din. "These people look like decent folks, but you never know what kind of trouble might be brewing."

Lise nodded, her gaze darting over the rowdy patrons. They reached the bar at last, wedging themselves into a gap between a pair of red-faced merchants. Danny leaned across the stained wood, trying to catch the eye of the sweating, bald bartender.

Minutes crawled by as servers came and went. Danny drummed his fingers against the bar as he waited. Finally, the bartender marched their way, a scowl etched onto his fleshy face.

"What'll it be?" he asked.

"A room with two beds for the night," Danny said. "And a bath, if you've got one."

The bartender squinted, taking in their road-stained

clothes and grim expressions. "Rooms are three silvers each. Bath's another two. Pay up front."

Danny slapped a small gold coin on the bar. "That do it?"

The bartender's scowl brightened as he scooped up the coin. "Yes, sir. Top of the stairs, last door on the left. I'll bring the tub once the lunch rush dies down. Probably an hour or so."

"That'll be fine, thanks." Danny pushed away from the bar and made his way to the stairs.

The room was small and spare, little more than a pair of narrow beds and a washstand. Danny crossed to the window, peering down at the street below. They still had plenty of daylight.

"Not much, but it'll do for a while." He turned back to Lise. She'd sat on the edge of one of the beds, hands folded in her lap. "Once they bring the tub, I'll head for the guild and see what I can learn. Don't worry, I'll leave a ward on the door."

"Thanks, for everything. I'm afraid I haven't been much use. It would've been easier for you to leave me behind."

"Easy and right are seldom the same thing. I have no regrets about my decision." Danny offered her his most reassuring smile. "I'll get you somewhere reasonably safe, I promise."

He dearly hoped that was a promise he could keep.

CHAPTER 8

Danny grunted as he and the bartender maneuvered a heavy metal tub through the doorway of his room. The damn thing had to weigh a couple hundred pounds. Physical enhancement magic made lifting it easy, but it was such an awkward shape. Three serving girls waited patiently in the hall behind them, each holding a steaming bucket of water.

Once they positioned the tub in the center of the room, the girls entered and emptied their buckets, sending plumes of steam billowing into the modest room. Danny wiped the sweat from his brow and surveyed their work with satisfaction. It wasn't much, but after weeks on the road, Lise deserved a hot bath at least.

Danny was quite looking forward to his turn as well.

He turned to Lise, who was much more interested in the tub than him. "I shouldn't be long. Be sure to bar the door behind me."

"I'll be fine, don't worry," Lise said. She sounded like she meant it, though he had his doubts.

Danny closed the door and paused until he heard the bar thunk into place. An effort of will conjured a ward that would paralyze anyone that tried to force the door open. Short of a death ward, this was as safe as he could make her.

"What's the big idea telling her to bar the door?" the bartender asked. "I run a safe place here."

"It's only prudent for a woman in the bath to take precautions. Where can I find the Adventurers' Guild?"

The bartender set out down the hall and Danny fell in beside him. "Out the door, turn left, two streets up turn right at the blacksmith's. It's two doors down from there. You can't miss it, they've got a big sign out front with a crossed sword and wand."

"Thanks for the directions and the tub. I'm sure Lise appreciates the latter as well."

"All part of the service," the bartender said with a distinct lack of enthusiasm. "Let me know when you get back and I'll have the girls change the water."

They reached the now much quieter common room and before heading for the door Danny said, "Will do."

Exiting the inn, Danny squinted against the afternoon sun. This time of year he figured he only had three hours of daylight left. Not wanting to waste any of it, he set off with purposeful strides down the street in the direction the bartender indicated.

As he passed groups of residents and merchants chatting, it seemed most of them were focused on plague rumors. Danny had no intention of poking his nose into a private conversation, but was curious to know what they were thinking. Panic hadn't set in yet, but he feared it was only a matter of time. The priests' efforts at the gates certainly helped.

It was harder to get worked up over the deaths of distant strangers than it was people you knew.

Before long, he found himself standing in front of the Adventurers' Guild. It wasn't all that impressive, and if it wasn't for the sign out front Danny would've walked right past. Nothing about its weathered wooden facade screamed that people with a lot of money came there regularly. On the covered front porch, a trio of armed men lounged in chairs near the door. They eyed him as he approached, one of them grinning like a madman. Hopefully they weren't the Redfield equivalent of Bruno.

Luckily, for them, they made no move to bother Danny as he pushed inside. He blinked a few times to help his eyes adjust to the relative dimness.

The main waiting area was smaller than the Rosenbar guild's, though it had the same basic layout. Only two parties were present, both of them enjoying a drink and paying Danny no attention. That was definitely an improvement over his first visit to the Rosenbar guild.

Danny made his way to the long wooden counter at the back of the room where two women a bit younger than Lise waited for customers. Danny stepped up to the counter and offered the nearest woman his best smile.

She responded in kind, displaying a mouthful of crooked teeth. "Are you looking to post a job, sir?"

Danny placed his guild badge on the counter. "Nope. I'm Ronin and I just arrived in town. I was hoping for some information on the plague. I took a sort of unofficial job with the mayor of White Hall to look into the source."

The secretary sighed, rubbing her eyes with ink-stained fingers. "There isn't much concrete news, I'm afraid, just rumors. No one seems to know where it came from, and only a powerful priest can cure it. Speaking of, the priests are doing their best to keep the stricken out of the city but there aren't enough of them to go from village to village."

Danny frowned. "Has anyone posted a job about it? Surely someone must be investigating the situation."

"There's been nothing I've seen. The average adventurer isn't equipped to handle a plague—bandits or Alpha Wolves, sure, but you can't stab a disease."

Danny couldn't argue with her. "I've heard Alpha Wolves mentioned before. What are they? They're not something that exists in the Five Kingdoms."

"They're really big wolves, like half the size of a draft horse. They travel in small groups rather than big packs. Worst of all, they have a taste for mutton. The Merchants' Guild has a standing bounty of five gold pieces on their skulls. Hunting them is the beastfolk's main occupation."

"They don't mind adventurers trying to get a cut?"

"There are plenty of Alpha Wolves to go around, more's the pity."

"Thanks for the help." He pocketed his badge and turned away from the counter.

He'd hoped for better intel, but she couldn't tell him what she didn't know. He'd take a quick look at the job board then head back. Lise should be done and a nice soak in a hot bath might jog some ideas loose.

A few quick strides carried him to the back wall where the job board waited. It wasn't overloaded with options. Bodyguard work, a notice about the bounties on Alpha Wolves that had "do not remove" written on it in large letters; nothing caught his eye or seemed plague related.

Looked like he'd have to find his answer elsewhere. His

best guess being with the beastfolk. He had no idea if there were any in the town, but he might get lucky.

Either way it was a job for tomorrow. Danny turned and walked out of the guild hall. The streets of Redfield were as crowded as when he entered, but he barely noticed the press of people as he retraced his steps toward the inn.

Halfway there, a shout cut through the clamor of the streets. "Cure for the plague! Get your cure for the plague here!"

Danny's head snapped around, his eyes narrowing as he scanned the crowd for the source of the voice. A charlatan peddling false hope, or something else? He couldn't dismiss the possibility of a cure out of hand, not with this world's magic.

At a minimum he needed to see what was going on.

○

The merchant's shouts grew louder as Danny wove through the bustling marketplace. He dodged carts laden with vegetables and narrowly avoided a collision with a burly man carrying a cage of squawking chickens. The air was thick with the mingled scents of spices, livestock, and unwashed bodies. The stink did nothing to discourage him as he got closer to his destination.

The idea of a potion that cured a plague as new as this one seemed absurd on its face, even with magic. He didn't have sufficient details to say for sure one way or the other.

He forced his way through the throng of shoppers and emerged in an open space where a covered wagon stood apart from the other stalls and shops. Two rough-looking guards in leather armor and armed with swords flanked the wagon. They had the hard look of men who knew how to fight. The wagon itself had a pullout table lined with blue potions.

Even from a distance he could sense the magic in the potions. At a bare minimum, they weren't complete frauds. The lack of customers was weird. No doubt the lack of sick and desperate people in Redfield wasn't great for business.

Maybe the merchant or whoever made the potion could tell him more about the plague. At this point, Danny wasn't about to overlook any potential source of information.

He approached the wagon, making sure to keep his hands well away from his weapon. As he drew nearer, the merchant, a short, chubby man with a long, curly mustache and richly embroidered tunic, turned his way. The merchant's eyes latched on to Danny like a drowning man to a rope.

"Welcome, sir!" The merchant waved Danny closer. "I can see you are a man of discerning taste. Surely you've heard of the miraculous cure I offer? For a mere ten gold coins, you can walk away with a vial of the most potent, not to mention only, plague remedy in the land. Guaranteed to banish the scourge from your body."

The merchant grabbed one of the vials and held it up to let the light play over the blue liquid. It was pretty if nothing else.

Ten gold coins was a high price. Danny had no idea what people around here made, but in the Five Kingdoms that would've covered three months' wages for the average laborer. Assuming they were talking small gold coins. If he meant large ones, it was closer to three years' wages.

"Tell me more about this potion of yours." Danny activated a lie detection spell. "Given your bold claims, I'm sure you can see why a person might be dubious."

"I understand your doubts, good sir. But I assure you, this potion has been rigorously tested by the esteemed temple of the Goddess, Lady of Healing. Their priests have confirmed its potency. Rest assured, anyone ill will soon be fully recovered."

Danny's eyebrows shot up. The temple of the Goddess was known for its integrity and devotion to the common good. If they vouched for his cure, then it must do what he claimed.

"I find it hard to believe the temple would approve of you selling it at such a high price. Most of the sick wouldn't be able to afford it. I assume that's why you're here rather than out in the villages offering your cure to actual victims."

The merchant winced, but quickly recovered. "The high price is a necessary evil, I'm afraid. The ingredients required to brew this potion are exceptionally rare and costly. You understand?"

Danny nodded. Time to try a different tactic. "Of course. There are always difficulties with this sort of thing."

The merchant blew out a breath of relief. "Exactly, sir. So, would you like a vial?"

"Maybe. The thing is, I'm not sick. Can you tell me how long the potion is viable? I'd hate to buy one only to find out when I get sick three months from now it's lost its potency."

The merchant shifted from foot to foot, reminding Danny of a little kid that had to pee. His eyes darted to his guards and back. "The thing is, sir, I am only a merchant, not the potion's creator. The alchemist that made it is the bashful sort, so he engaged the service of myself and several other merchants to sell his wares. We split the profits fifty-fifty."

So far the merchant hadn't lied. He likely also hadn't revealed everything he knew either.

Much as Danny wanted to get to the bottom of the mystery, pushing the issue further might lead to trouble. The guards' hands were drifting toward their sword hilts and the merchant looked on the verge of a nervous breakdown. While Danny had no doubt he could deal with these two without breaking a sweat, causing a scene would only make his task more difficult. At worst it might end up with him and Lise getting thrown out of Redfield. That wasn't something he wanted to risk.

It was time to back off, at least for now. Just to be safe, he put an ethereal marker on the wagon. He'd be able to track it wherever it went.

"I appreciate you taking the time to answer my questions. Unfortunately, without knowing how long the potion is good for, I'll have to pass. When you talk to the alchemist again, you might want to ask about those sorts of details. I'm sure your future customers would appreciate it. Good afternoon."

With that, Danny turned on his heel and strode back toward the inn. He didn't know what was going on, but the whole thing stunk to high heaven.

Maybe it would make more sense after a hot bath and a meal. And even if it didn't, he'd still feel better.

CHAPTER 9

Danny woke up and stretched. For the first time in far too long, he felt rested and clean. The money he spent on that bath was the best investment ever. He allowed himself ten seconds to revel before turning his thoughts to the merchant. No great epiphany had come to him during the night, but he had no doubt there was something going on with the guy. Who would try to sell a product they basically knew nothing about?

The answer, obviously, was that guy. He had to be counting on desperation to move units. The merchant might've been a sleazeball, but the alchemist that made the potions interested Danny more. The problem was he had no idea who he was or where to find him.

So many questions and so few answers.

First things first. Danny opened himself to the ether and sent his awareness out. It took only a moment to confirm the wagon's presence. In fact, it hadn't moved at all. On the one hand, that was good, since Danny had more research to do.

On the other hand, if the merchant had left, Danny could've tracked him to wherever his supplier worked.

He released the spell and swung his legs out of bed. As he was slipping his feet into his boots, Lise stirred and opened her eyes. "What's the plan for today?"

"I'm going to visit the temple of the Goddess. See if I can learn anything more about those plague potions."

"Can I come?" Lise pushed herself up. "Sitting around here all day wondering what's happening doesn't appeal to me. Gives me too much time to think."

He hesitated for a moment before nodding. The town was peaceful and visiting the temple should be safe. "Sure. We'll head out as soon as you're ready."

Danny stepped into the hall to give her a bit of privacy. Unlike women from his world, Lise didn't need long to get ready and five minutes later they were on their way downstairs to the common room.

The breakfast rush Danny had expected was nowhere to be seen. In fact, the tables were empty save for a trio of serving girls eating their own breakfasts. One moved to stand up and wait on them, but Danny waved her off and headed for the bar.

The bartender emerged from the kitchen and stomped over. "Need something?"

Danny set three small silver coins on the bar. "The room for another night."

The bartender shook his head. "Your coins are too small. Don't recognize the mint, but that's not going to do it."

"Is there a moneychanger around here? I need some local currency."

"I can help with that, for a ten percent fee."

Danny rubbed the bridge of his nose. He had no idea if that was fair but he had so much wealth from working with Lyra he could afford it. "Fine. Say, if there's no lord, who handles minting the local coin?"

"Merchants' Guild." The bartender reached under the bar and came up with a scale and three lead coins of various sizes. "You have to be a member to change coins. How much did you want to do?"

Danny had two large gold coins in his satchel and placed them on the bar. "Give me one in gold and the other silver."

The bartender took Danny's coins and got busy. In the end he ended up with seven gold coins and seventy silvers after the bartender took his cut.

As Danny was picking up his money the bartender said, "Thanks for your business. I'll even give you the room for half off tonight."

"Thanks." Danny gave him two silver coins. "Where can I find the temple of the Goddess?"

"You feeling sick?" The bartender looked down at his hands as if expecting them to start rotting off.

"No, you can relax." Danny told him about his encounter with the potion merchant the day before. "I want to know more about what he's selling. I figure if anyone can tell me about those potions, whoever inspected them can."

"I heard about that guy. Some of the regulars were laughing about him last night. What kind of idiot sells a cure where no one's sick? Anyway, the temples are in the north-west quarter not far from the gate. The Goddess's is the biggest, you can't miss it."

"Thanks." Despite his manner, the bartender didn't seem like such a bad guy. "Ready?"

Lise nodded and followed him outside. The air had a

bite to it despite the bright sunlight. Hopefully the snow would hold off for a bit longer. The street was already bustling with farmers and merchants driving their wagons toward the market. Plague or not, business went on.

The savory scent of cooking meat drew him to a busy stall up the street from the Golden Gate. The source of the aroma was a grill covered with bursting sausages. They were served on skewers so you could eat as you walked. Kind of like meat lollipops.

Danny got in line and when his turn came said, "Two please."

The vendor skewered his order and traded them for one of Danny's newly acquired silver coins. He handed one to Lise and they turned west, keeping to the edge of the road so as not to get run over by wagons.

They ate as they walked, the rich, spiced meat doing wonders to lift Danny's spirits. Halfway through Danny said, "Not bad."

"No, not bad at all," Lise agreed. "Though I feel a bit guilty relying on you to pay for everything."

"Don't worry about it. One more person doesn't add all that much cost and I enjoy the company."

She gave him a bashful smile that made some of the years melt off her face. He wasn't just saying that to make her feel better. Traveling alone, while faster, would've been way less interesting.

Redfield wasn't a huge town and by the time they finished their breakfast they were standing in front of the Goddess's temple. It was a modest stone building, its only embellishment a stained-glass window depicting a winged woman above the heavy oak door. Danny grasped the iron handle and found it unlocked. He pushed through into the warm chapel.

He rubbed his hands. The heat felt good after the morning chill. There was no stove so he assumed magic heated the building. So much divine energy filled the air that he couldn't locate the source of the heat.

In the chapel, rows of wooden pews led to an altar at the front, where a priest in white robes adorned with a red cross polished candle holders with a dirty rag.

He smiled at their approach, his weathered face brightening. "Welcome, strangers. My name is Father Sander. How may I assist you today?"

Danny returned the smile and strode down the aisle. "I'm Ronin and this is Lise. I was hoping you could tell me about the plague potions. Are you the one who analyzed them?"

Father Sander's smile soured. "Ah yes, those things. I am, indeed, the one who analyzed them. A dubious honor indeed. I'm afraid there's not much I can tell you. They work, though the price borders on extortion."

"How long are they good for?"

The priest spread his hands in a helpless gesture. "I wish I could say, but all my magic revealed is that the potions are indeed effective against the plague. Though I disapprove of the price, it's not the church's place to deny anyone the right to conduct business. If a wealthy person should come down with the plague, a potion could save them. That's reason enough not to interfere."

"Right, thanks Father." Danny handed him a small gold coin. "Here, a small donation to the greater good."

"The Goddess watch over you."

"May she watch over us all." Danny turned and strode out of the temple.

"That didn't amount to much," Lise said.

"Nope." Danny blew out a sigh. "We need a new plan. There has to be someone in this town who knows something about those damned potions."

"And if there isn't?"

He didn't have an answer for her. Much as he wanted to bring the plague to an end, there was only so much he could do.

"Let's take a walk. Clear our heads."

Lise fell into step beside him and together they walked down the street. Danny had no particular destination in mind and that was the problem. He was a stranger in this town. He had no friends and no contacts, no one he could ask for help.

Maybe the beastfolk knew something. He could go hunting for Alpha Wolves and hope he ran into a fellow hunter. At a minimum it would be better than wandering around at random, hoping for inspiration to strike.

O

Osbern carefully set a crate of potions aside, the vials clinking as he did, and rubbed his pudgy hands together to warm them. The crates took up so much space in the back of his wagon he barely had room to lie down at night. Luckily, in town that wasn't an issue. He'd enjoyed a nice, warm bed in a fine inn last night. Of course, if he didn't start selling some potions, that was going to change in the not-too-distant future.

Grumbling, he opened the wagon's hidden compartment and pulled out the crystal ball his partner had provided. Osbern grimaced. He liked to think of the rather grim alchemist as his partner in the business of selling potions, but the truth was, Osbern was at best a junior partner and at worst a servant. Much as he hated to think of it that way, it didn't change the truth. He didn't even know the man's name for heaven's sake!

As long as he ended up rich, Osbern was willing to play second fiddle. But for the moment, not only was he a servant, he was a poor one. That wouldn't do at all.

He set the crystal ball on a three-legged stool and offered a weary sigh that shook his considerable girth. He stared at his distorted reflection in the crystal for a moment. No matter how long he waited, this wasn't going to get any easier.

Taking a deep breath, Osbern placed his stubby fingers on the orb's cool surface. He pictured the alchemist's angular, almost skeletal face. A face, he hated to admit, that scared the ever-living hell out of him.

Seconds passed before the crystal shimmered, swirling with an eerie light. Osbern sat up, tugging his embroidered tunic straight. He pasted on an ingratiating smile as the alchemist's gaunt face appeared, floating in the orb's depths.

"Why do you trouble me? Surely you can handle selling potions to peasants."

"Right, you see, Master, no one wants to buy the potions. There are no sick people in Redfield after all. I'm uncertain what to do." Osbern bowed his head in deference, swallowing the many complaints he wanted to offer.

The alchemist's voice slithered through Osbern's mind, a harsh snarl that sent shivers down his spine. "Not an unexpected result given the circumstances. Now that you've established yourself and your story, when those circumstances change, you will be poised to profit."

Osbern lit up at the word profit, but that only lasted a moment. "I don't understand, Master."

"The health of the local populace is about to take a turn for the worse. Be patient and be ready."

Osbern had no idea how the alchemist would sneak an infected person into the town, not with a priest manning each gate day and night. "Of course, Master. Rest assured I'll be ready."

He hesitated, debating whether to mention the overly curious fellow from the previous day.

"If you have something to say, say it. I have other matters that require my attention."

"Yes, Master. There was one small matter, an adventurer, asking questions about the potion. I had no idea how to answer him."

The alchemist's eyes narrowed. "Did this adventurer interfere with your business?"

"No, Master," Osbern said. "But he struck me as the sort of person who might cause problems."

"If he becomes a hindrance, eliminate him. That's why I provided you with warriors. In any case, one man is no threat to my plans."

"Yes, Master. All shall be as you say."

"Indeed it shall." The alchemist's face faded from the crystal ball.

Osbern slumped back, leaning against a crate. His heart pounded and he feared that conversation had shaved a year off his life.

Had he made the right decision, going into business with the alchemist? Osbern had his doubts, but there was no backing out now, not if he wanted to enjoy a long life with his soon-to-be-acquired wealth. It was too late for second-guessing now. He was in too deep, and there was no turning back.

Besides, thanks to the alchemist's magic, he was now immune to the plague. That alone was worth the risk, assuming the disease continued to spread the way he expected. Indeed, Osbern was a lucky fellow.

CHAPTER 10

D anny stood in a frost-covered field, his breath misting in the cold air. The crunch of brittle grass underfoot echoed across the empty expanse as he gazed down the Western Trade Road, now just a distant ribbon on the horizon. Lise hadn't been thrilled when he said he was going out on his own to try and make contact with the beastfolk, but bringing her on an Alpha Wolf hunt was a way different thing than taking her to the temple of the Goddess.

Besides, he would be covering a lot of ground today and using his magic to speed up the process. There was no way she could've kept up. The pouch of coins he'd left her should last her a week or so. Danny hoped to be back well before that, but he'd been hunting enough times to know there were no guarantees.

Putting Lise out of his mind, Danny opened himself fully to the ether. After a minute of searching it became clear that the only life forms nearby were the humans in Redfield. The Alpha Wolves, it appeared, lived further afield.

Oh well, he hadn't expected to get lucky on his first try. Finding the Alpha Wolves was never going to be easy and even if he succeeded there was no way to know if there would be beastfolk in the area. In all his wandering Danny hadn't seen a single member of that race in Redfield.

Danny sighed. He needed to put some more miles between himself and civilization. He turned northwest and ran. Ether flowed through him and he managed a solid ten miles in an hour. In all that time he saw nothing beyond endless rolling hills. At least the temperature had gone up a bit. Between that and the jog he was almost warm.

A few minutes with the searching spell confirmed he was alone out here. Even if there were no wolves or hunters, he thought he might've run into some shepherds. This looked like good grazing land to Danny, not that he was any sort of expert on sheep fodder.

He'd covered fifty miles by the time noon arrived. Danny paused under a rare shade tree and took some jerky out of his storage. He gnawed on the tough meat and let his awareness drift. There had to be some beastfolk around here somewhere.

The thought had barely formed when he sensed four nonhuman life forces. Not wanting to miss his chance, Danny hurried toward them. A mile later he spotted a group of three beastfolk hunters. One of them was lying on the ground, unmoving, while the other two fought a wolf the size of an adult horse.

Its fangs flashed as it lunged at the hunters. Somehow they dodged but it was a near thing. The woman at the Adventurers' Guild said Alpha Wolves were half the size of a horse. He didn't know what this was.

And it didn't matter. If he didn't step in, he wouldn't have a chance to talk with the beastfolk.

Danny rushed forward, closing to spell range.

Shaping the ether, Danny unleashed a blast of lightning. The bolt hammered into the wolf's side, staggering the beast and giving the hunters a moment to gather themselves.

Suspicious glances darted Danny's way before the battle was rejoined. His spell hadn't done the beast any serious damage, which told him a great deal about how tough it was.

Taking a few seconds, Danny gathered three times as much power and hurled a crackling blast that sent the wolf tumbling backwards as it howled in pain.

The hunters took advantage of the moment, driving their spears deep into the wolf's flanks.

The wolf howled again as blood stained its gray coat red.

Danny formed a fist of ether and brought it down on the beast's head, breaking its neck and ending the fight.

He blew out a breath. That had been too close.

Danny turned his attention to the injured beastman. The hunter lay on the ground, his leg torn and bloody from the Alpha Wolf's bite. His companions stood between him and Danny, their expressions a mix of worry and suspicion.

Now that things had calmed down, Danny had a chance to look closer at the beastfolk. They looked generally human. Only the wolflike ears, thick hair on their calves and fore- arms, and tails were different.

"I can help him," Danny said. "Please, let me heal his wounds."

The wounded hunter grabbed one of his fellow's legs. When the hunter looked down, the beastman nodded.

The hunters hesitated a moment longer, then inched away

to let Danny kneel beside their injured companion. Placing his hands over the wound, Danny flooded it with holy energy. He watched as the flesh regenerated and skin reformed.

A little over a minute later the wound was gone. The hunter would be weak for a while, but he would recover.

"Thank you," the healed beastman said, his voice a little growly but still intelligible. "We owe you a debt."

Danny grinned. "If you'd be willing to talk with me a bit, we'll call it even."

He shifted and sat facing the now recovered hunter. The others settled on either side of their companion.

"My name is Darmin," the newly healed hunter said. "Who are you? And what brings you so far from the human villages?"

"I'm Ronin, an adventurer. I was asked by the mayor of White Hall to look into the plague that's been spreading through the human population. I couldn't find anything useful in Redfield beyond a sketchy merchant selling cure potions. One of the victims mentioned encountering a beast-folk hunter before he fell ill. With no better ideas, I figured I'd see if your people had any idea where the disease came from."

The hunters exchanged glances and Darmin said, "We know of no plague, at least not in our pack. Our clan chief recently traveled north to the annual pack meet. It's possible he learned something there. I will introduce you if you wish."

Danny nodded. "I would very much appreciate that. One more thing, if you don't mind. It's not related to my search, but according to the secretary at the guild, Alpha Wolves were supposed to be half the size of the one we fought. Was I misled?"

"No. These creatures are new." Darmin snarled, baring his

fangs. "They came out of the north. An aggressive subspecies, the shaman says. All I know is they're tougher than the regular wolves. Two teams of hunters have been wiped out by them in the last three weeks. It would've been three if you hadn't arrived when you did."

Danny frowned. Sounded like there were some issues further north. Though still a long ways away, Elfhome was generally northwest of here. Hopefully the elves' capital wasn't related to the current troubles.

"How far is it to your pack?" Danny asked.

"Perhaps a day. We don't range as far as we used to with the new wolves wandering around. Speaking of which, take the wolf as a thank-you gift. Its pelt will fetch a good price in the markets, and its meat will feed you for many days."

"It was a team effort. What say I take the pelt and you keep the meat for your pack?"

Darmin nodded. "An honorable offer. It is agreed."

The hunter held out his hand and when Danny went to grasp it he twisted so they gripped at an angle like they were getting ready to arm wrestle.

Everyone stood. Danny went over to the giant wolf and opened his storage under it. The carcass sank out of sight into his pocket dimension. The hunters watched with wide eyes. Perhaps they had never seen such a thing. It was supposed to be a pretty rare skill after all.

"Are we ready?" Darmin asked.

Danny nodded and the group set out at a jog. Hopefully the pack leader would have some information for Danny. If not, he wasn't sure what his next move would be.

L ise perched at the edge of the narrow bed, her gaze fixed on the uneven floorboards. Ronin had only been gone for a few hours and already she didn't know what to do with herself. It was pathetic. At some point, certainly far sooner than she would've liked, they were going to part company for good. If she was this much of a mess after a few hours, how would she manage the rest of her life?

She thought back to their first meeting. Ronin had asked her if she wanted to live and she'd said yes. And she'd meant it. For the first time since her family was taken, she realized she did indeed want to live.

But had she been living? Following on Ronin's coattails and letting him handle everything hardy felt like a proper life. Sometimes Lise felt more like a pet than a person. That Ronin never treated her like one made her like him more than she should. They had no future as anything but friends, he'd made that clear.

And she was okay with that. Her lips quirked in a humorless smile. Okay, not really, but she did understand reality however little she liked it. This time alone was a good chance to try and figure some things out. The main one being how she was going to survive once she was on her own.

The only job Lise had ever had was wife. That covered a lot of ground. She could cook, look after children, and manage a household. Years of hard work and travel had left her strong with plenty of stamina. Lise figured she could do plenty of jobs.

"Right!" she said.

Maybe she wasn't going to stay in Redfield long term, but that made it the perfect place to practice. And this inn would be a good place to begin. Surely they had need of help. She remembered how busy it had been when she first arrived.

Lise hopped off the bed and headed for the hall. Maybe the bartender would say no and tell her off. She was prepared for that. She didn't need the money right now. This was a test to see if she could manage on her own.

A short walk down the steps brought her to the common room. The aroma of roasting meat mingled with the sharp tang of spilled ale. There were only three patrons at the moment. As she'd hoped, the lunch rush hadn't begun. That this area even had lunch was strange to her. In the Five Kingdoms it was a rare treat to eat a noon meal.

She went right to the bar where the man she assumed either owned or managed the place was rearranging the bottles on the back wall. "Excuse me."

The bartender turned to face her. He seemed basically incapable of smiling though today's glower was a bit less severe than usual. "Need something?"

"A job. Have any openings?"

"A job?" His incredulous tone annoyed her but she didn't let it show. "Your man not taking good care of you?"

"Ronin isn't my man. He saved my life and has been kind enough to serve as my escort. If we're going to be in Redfield for a while I want to do my part to cover expenses. So, do you have a job or not?"

"Don't need any barmaids, but I could use a hand in the kitchen. Can you cook?"

"Long as you don't want anything too fancy."

He cracked a smile and laughed. "Take a look around. We don't do fancy here. You work in the kitchen and I'll cover the cost of your room. Deal?"

Lise smiled back. It wasn't like she needed money. "Deal."

"You'd best get started." The bartender pointed at the

door to the kitchen. "There's a pile of potatoes in there that won't peel themselves."

Lise didn't let her excitement show, but it felt good to take this step. She couldn't wait to see the look on Ronin's face when he got back.

It felt like things were finally going her way.

CHAPTER 11

Sunset was approaching when Danny and the beastfolk hunters crested a rise. A cluster of hide tents sat beside a grassy mound, and tendrils of smoke rising from a central fire pit curled into the sky. It reminded Danny of historical pictures of Plains Natives back home. The tents even looked like teepees.

Darmin held up a hand and the hunters halted. Figures came trotting up from the camp to intercept them, spears raised and ready.

"Everything okay?" Danny asked.

"This is a standard precaution," Darmin said. "The females and young are here, so we have to be careful who we let approach. Beastfolk seldom enter another pack's territory, but mate raids aren't unknown."

"Who's there?" the lead beastman asked, his yellow eyes flashing as he glared at Danny.

"It's Darmin. We've returned from the hunt. This human helped us take down one of the new Alpha Wolves. He also saved my life. Ronin is a friend."

The sentries lowered their weapons. "Very well. We honor your wisdom, Hunt Leader."

Danny and the hunters made their way down into the makeshift village while the guards went back on patrol. Danny was keenly aware of the stares tracking his every move. About twenty adult beastfolk milled about, mostly females. Aside from their curves, the women had the same wiry, muscular physique as the men, only smaller.

The younger hunters hurried over and embraced what he assumed were their mates. A handful of kids stared up at Danny before being shooed back inside the huts.

Seemed like a peaceful life. Everyone looked fit and healthy. Certainly there was no sign of the plague. Danny was less reassured than he might've been given his theory that the beastfolk were immune. Well, he had his holy aura active, so even if they all had the disease, it wouldn't trouble him.

Darmin led him to the center of the camp where a massive beastman stood waiting, his bare chest latticed with old scars. He regarded Danny with intense amber eyes.

"Rafe," Darmin said. "This is Ronin. He helped us kill one of the new Alpha Wolves, saving our lives in the process. Ronin, Rafe is our pack leader."

Danny nodded, meeting Rafe's penetrating gaze. "Good to meet you. I was pleased I reached Darmin and his companions in time. I've never seen a wolf the size of that thing."

"They are a new menace," Rafe said. "As if life didn't demand enough already. Fortunately there are few of them in our territory. Regular Alpha Wolves we can handle without issue."

"Speaking of." Danny opened his storage and let the giant wolf carcass fall on the ground. "Dinner's my treat."

"We offered Ronin the pelt and skull in gratitude for his effort," Darmin said.

"An excellent trade for us," Rafe said. "This much meat will last the pack for weeks."

Six beastwomen gathered around the carcass, curved knives in hand, ready to butcher the kill. As they set to work stripping the hide and carving meat, Danny turned back to Rafe. "I was hoping we could talk."

Rafe nodded. "Of course. While they prepare dinner, we can discuss whatever brings you so far from human territory. Even the shepherds seldom come this far from the villages. This way."

Rafe led them a little ways from the butcher before he sat on the ground. Danny and Darmin joined him. There was no particular ceremony about it. Just three men sitting and talking. Danny found that comforting.

"What's on your mind?" Rafe asked.

"The plague." Danny shared everything he'd learned so far. "Have you heard anything about it?"

"Hmm…" Rafe turned and waved. "Sybil, come join us please."

An elderly beastwoman, her fur streaked with white, strode over and eased down beside them. "How may I advise you, Pack Leader?"

"This is Sybil, shaman of our pack," Rafe said. "Sybil, meet Ronin, the human who aided our hunters today."

Danny inclined his head. "Pleasure, ma'am."

He sensed no magic about her. Looked like she was what she seemed: an old beastwoman steeped in the knowledge of her people.

Rafe repeated what Danny had told him. "Does it mean anything to you?"

"Our people have always been strong. Disease is never an issue for us. That is a human weakness."

"Could this illness be the cause of the absences at the pack gathering?" Rafe asked.

"Doubtful," Sybil said. "As I said, we don't get sick."

"What's the gathering about?" It was probably a long shot that it had anything to do with the plague, but Danny was getting desperate.

"An annual meeting when many packs come together to arrange mate swaps. It brings fresh blood into the family. Seven packs didn't attend," Rafe said. "All from the northern territories. We've never had a gathering where so many didn't attend."

"What's to the north of here?" Danny asked. "Beyond the territories of the absent packs?"

The pack leader shook his shaggy head. "I don't know. It's taboo for us to enter another pack's territory. I know mate raids happen, but that's only one or two reckless youths."

"Surely someone must know something," Danny said. "Tales, old legends, anything would be helpful."

"Our pack has never ventured to those lands," Sybil said. "We would not be welcome if we did. A lone human, however, might pass through unnoticed. If there is danger, it would be good to know before it reached our pack."

"Sybil!" Rafe said. "Ronin is our guest and we already owe him for saving Darmin and his team. We can ask for nothing more."

"That's okay," Danny said. "This is the only lead I have. Even if it ends up unrelated to the plague, I need to make sure. If I can help your pack in the process, I'm happy to do so."

"I will go with you," Darmin said. "To repay my debt."

"I appreciate the offer," Danny said. "But if we're caught, having you along could cause trouble for your pack. Better if I go alone. Should I learn anything, I'll return."

Danny's stomach rumbled as the scent of roasting meat wafted through the camp, drawing a laugh from Rafe. "Enough talk. Let us eat. Wolf meat will make you strong for your journey."

He wasn't sure what to think about eating wolf meat. Some cultures back home ate dog so this was sort of the same thing. He also didn't want to be rude to his hosts. Wouldn't hurt to give it a try.

A group of beastwomen brought over plates of rare steak. Blood pooled around it and there were no utensils. Danny didn't consider himself a picky eater, but this was pushing it. The beastfolk were tearing chunks out of the meat and eating it without issue.

Drawing on the ether, Danny sent heat into the steak until the flesh sizzled and browned. He pulled out his knife, cut off a reasonable-sized bite, and popped it in his mouth. It was tough and kind of gamey, but not inedible.

"You ruined it," Rafe said.

Danny swallowed and said, "Humans have different tastes."

When the meal was finished, the hunters brought Rafe a bundle of fur with a skull on top. "The pelt and skull, as promised."

"Thank you." Danny accepted the pelt and put it in storage. "It will bring me a good price in Redfield."

"Rest with us tonight," Rafe said. "The plains are even more dangerous at night."

Danny couldn't argue with that. Not to mention he was beat. "I accept your hospitality, thank you."

They didn't have a spare tent for him so Danny spread his bedroll out by the fire. The heat was nice. Hopefully it would linger until morning. Once he got back to Redfield, he needed to do some research and try to figure out what was north of here and whether it would be best to take Lise with him or leave her where it was safe.

He yawned. Those questions would keep. Danny set a silent ward around the camp, closed his eyes, and soon fell sound asleep.

CHAPTER 12

Danny jolted awake. The ward he placed around the camp had been triggered. A moment later someone screamed.

He leapt to his feet. Figures with torches were running through the dark. Two teepees were already burning. By the flickering light of the flames what looked like human warriors dressed in leather armor were busy tying up an unmoving beastman. Two kids lay equally still beside him.

Danny snarled and summoned globes of light, turning night into day.

Everywhere he turned rough-looking men darted between the teepees, clubs and swords flashing in their hands. Why were humans raiding a beastfolk camp? As far as Danny could tell they had nothing of value to humans.

That was a question he could answer later. For now, dealing with the warriors was his priority.

Danny drew his sword and activated his physical enhancements. Kicking off the ground hard, he charged toward the nearest trio of men as the torchbearer was about to light another teepee on fire.

The nearest man's eyes widened when he saw Danny. A moment later his head went flying.

The second man's iron club blocked Danny's first swing, but a follow-up thrust took him through the throat. The torchbearer didn't last much longer and soon Danny was looking for new targets.

Hunters were emerging from undamaged teepees, spears in hand. They lunged into the melee, howling for blood.

Danny turned his focus to the bound prisoners. Four men stood over a handful of beastwomen and kids. They shifted to meet Danny.

Not wanting to risk collateral damage, Danny hit them with an arc of lightning that jumped from one iron club to the next until all the men collapsed in a twitching heap.

"Fall back!" The order came from somewhere beyond Danny's light. "Fall back now!"

No way was he going to let the bastards escape so they could try again some other night. A powerful, magic-assisted leap carried him across the camp in a single bound. Light exploded out at his command, revealing a group of fleeing soldiers. Danny thrust a hand out, unleashing a wave of pure force, an invisible sledgehammer that caught them from behind and sent them tumbling.

A howl went up from behind. The beastfolk came roaring out of their camp toward the unconscious men.

Shit! They needed at least one of them alive or they'd never figure out where they came from.

"Rafe!" Danny shouted. "Stop! We need them alive. Rafe!"

"Hold!" Rafe said.

By some miracle the enraged hunters obeyed. They circled the unconscious men, snarling and growling.

Rafe strode over to Danny. "Why would you spare them?"

"These men aren't here for fun. They've got a purpose. The clubs and ropes make it clear they wanted prisoners. I thought it might be good to know why and more importantly who sent them. We can't ask them if they're dead. One of this lot gave the order to retreat. That makes him the leader. If anyone's going to know the details, he will."

Rafe gave a full-body shake. "You make a good point. My people are not always wise when we're angry. I desire these answers as well."

Danny clapped him on the shoulder. "Would you have your hunters tie them up? There's plenty of rope. I'm going to check on the injured. Those clubs can do plenty of damage. If any of the hunters were hurt in the fight, have them join me."

It was a short walk back to the unconscious women and kids. Sybil knelt beside them. The old shaman looked up as he approached. "At the rate you're going, our pack will never be able to repay you."

Danny smiled. "I'm glad I could help. And don't worry about repaying me. Dealing with people that would beat a kid unconscious is its own reward. Hang on."

He channeled holy energy into the unmoving figures. The white glow lasted only a few seconds before they sat up, fully recovered. Good, their injuries couldn't have been too bad if the spell worked that quickly.

The women grabbed their little ones and hugged them. Danny was glad he could help them. They seemed like good people and he hated the idea of anyone harming them.

Rafe approached and said, "The prisoners are secure and none of the hunters are in need of healing."

That was a surprise. "None of them were hurt? I'm impressed."

Rafe bared his fangs. "A few cuts will leave nice scars to remind us to take our security more seriously. Will you question them now or wait until morning?"

"Now. I won't be able to sleep until I know what's going on. Do you mind playing the bad guard?"

Rafe cocked his head. "The what?"

"Basically I'll act nice and reasonable while pointing out that if they don't cooperate they'll have to deal with you, the angry pack leader who wants to eat them."

"We don't eat humans."

"As a human, I appreciate that. However, the threat of being eaten invokes a primal fear in people that will hopefully prove motivating. You don't actually have to carry the threat out."

"I'll do my best," Rafe said. "Let's get this over with."

That sounded like an excellent idea to Danny. He led the way over to the prisoners, who sat in a circle, their hands tied behind their backs, overseen by a group of scowling hunters. Perfect, they were doing a great job setting the mood.

"Okay," Danny said. "Who's in charge? I don't want to accidentally kill the wrong person."

All he got was a bunch of sullen glares in reply. Pity they weren't going to be reasonable.

"Is that the way it's going to be?" he asked. "Are you all willing to die for whoever sent you? My friends need to stock up on meat for the winter, so that's convenient for them, but personally I'd prefer to punish the person pulling your strings."

Danny crouched in front of an especially muscular prisoner and poked his bicep. "How much do you think this one would yield?"

"Maybe seventy pounds of lean meat plus the organs." Rafe shrugged. "Ninety pounds total. Should last us about a week."

"What do you want to know!?" one of them shouted. "Please, I'll tell you anything, just keep those savages away from me."

"Shut up, Peter!" another one shouted.

Bingo, he had to be the leader. But for now Danny would focus on Peter. He moved over to face the trembling young man. "It's always nice to meet a reasonable man. Who sent you?"

"I don't know his name," Peter said. "The captain assigned us to work for this creepy wizard. He's got the company doing all sorts of jobs, guard duty, slave raids, scouting, you name it. The money's good and it's better than fighting a war. Easiest job we've had since joining the guild."

"You've done this before?" Danny's voice had an edge that drew a flinch from Peter.

"A couple times. The other groups didn't put up much of a fight. Of course they didn't have a wizard with them either. What's a human doing hanging around with beastfolk anyway?"

"That's hardly your concern," Danny said. "Where did you take your prisoners?"

"To the wizard. He's set up in an old elf-blood outpost north of here about two hundred miles. We already picked up all the nearby groups."

"The captain's going to kill you, Peter," said the man Danny assumed was the leader.

"Rafe, would you shut him up, please?"

"With pleasure." The pack leader strode over, grabbed the man's chin in one hand and his skull in the other. A single hard twist broke his neck with a loud crack.

Danny had been hoping he'd knock the man out, but that worked too. "Now that the distractions have been dealt with…"

Peter had gotten very pale and looked like he was about to faint.

Danny gave him a smack. "Hey! Focus. Don't you dare pass out on me."

"He killed Sergeant Casper." Peter barely choked the words out.

"Yes, and if you don't want to end up the same, you need to pay attention and answer my questions. What is the wizard doing with the prisoners?"

"Working them in the fields. Beastfolk have a lot of stamina and they never get sick. They make great slaves. It's not like they're good for anything else." Peter blanched further when the hunters growled. "I probably shouldn't have said that last bit."

"Probably not, but I appreciate your honesty. You mentioned a guild. I assume that would be the Mercenaries' Guild."

"Yes, sir. The Discourt guild."

Danny didn't recognize the name but assumed it was one of the unlabeled cities on his map west of here. "Last questions, how big is your company, who leads it, and what is it called?"

"Two hundred men, mostly infantry with thirty archers

and ten scouts. Our captain's name is Koch and we're called Koch's Raiders."

"No magic users?" Danny asked.

"No, sir. Captain Koch couldn't afford to hire one."

Danny nodded. He'd learned all he needed. "Do what you like with them."

"Wait!" Peter said. "You said if I talked, you'd spare us."

"No, I said the beastfolk wouldn't eat you. And they won't. I promise."

At Rafe's command the hunters ran the men through. It was a quicker death than they deserved, but Danny was relieved to have it over with.

"Everything comes back to the north," Rafe said. "What will you do?"

"I need to return to Redfield and see if the Adventurers' Guild knows anything. Once I finish my research I'll head north and take a look around. If I can free the beastfolk, I will. I'd also like to have a word with this wizard and see if he knows anything about the plague."

Rafe chuffed a laugh at that. "I doubt such a person will be eager to talk to you."

"He'll talk to me, eager or not."

CHAPTER 13

Danny blinked the stickiness out of his eyes and sat up on his bedroll. His head was swearing at him after his broken sleep. He couldn't decide if he felt better or worse after the last four hours. He settled on better, mostly because no one had shown up and tried to kill them. That was a vast improvement over last night's violence.

He pushed himself up on one elbow and took a look around. The bodies of the mercenaries were gone. Whatever the hunters had done with them, he didn't care. It was just a relief not to have to look at them. He'd seen enough bodies to last him a lifetime and feared he'd be seeing plenty more before his mission was complete. Danny much preferred fighting demons. They were tougher, but once you killed them they disappeared on their own.

Danny sighed and stood. A little holy energy channeled through his body did wonders to wipe away the aches and pains. Eve warned him against relying on healing magic for such minor issues, but Danny saw no sense in suffering unnecessarily.

Anyway, Danny needed to get going. Preferably before the beastfolk felt the need to offer him any leftover wolf meat for breakfast. But first he wanted to have a quick word with Rafe.

Speaking of, Rafe emerged from his teepee just as Danny was thinking of him. Hoping to catch him before he got busy, Danny hurried over.

"Good morning, Ronin," Rafe said. "Will you be leaving us today?"

"Yup, as soon as I can get my things together. I've got a lot to do in Redfield before I head north. You'll probably want to take some extra precautions after last night."

"I plan to, starting with moving our camp to a new, more secure location. A place we've never met another pack. If the human soldiers want to take another crack at us, they'll have to find us first. Also, before you go I want to thank you again for your help last night. If not for you, I don't know what might've happened."

"I was glad to do it." Danny held out his hand and they shook. "I wish you and your pack the best of luck."

"The same to you. Know that you will get a warm welcome should you visit us."

Danny nodded and went back to his resting place to gather his stuff. It didn't take long to roll up his bedroll and strap it to his pack. Once his sword was buckled on he was good to go.

As Danny started walking, he was surprised to find the entire pack had emerged from their teepees to wave good-bye. It was a nice gesture and he felt a little emotional leaving them behind. Hopefully he could straighten things out so they wouldn't face any more nights like the last one.

At the edge of camp he found Darmin waiting, spear in hand and a small pack over his shoulder.

"You don't have to come, Darmin," Danny said. "I know my way back."

"Maybe, but you shouldn't travel alone. It's not safe for anyone."

It was way safer for Danny than it would be for anyone else, but if Darmin wanted to tag along, Danny wouldn't turn down the company.

"If you insist, let's go."

With Darmin at his side, Danny turned south. It was a few miles to the Western Trade Road, but once they reached it they could make better time.

Or so he thought. They'd barely got going when Darmin turned east.

"Where are you going?" Danny asked.

"Shortcut. If we cut cross country between the hills, it'll shorten the trip by hours. I hunt this area all the time. Don't worry, I won't get us lost."

One thing you learned in the Marines was not to ignore your local guide. If Darmin said this route would be faster, Danny was willing to trust him.

They hurried on at a ground-devouring lope, seeing nothing but grass and the occasional scattered clump of trees. It was somewhat disconcerting, like the two of them were the only people in the world. It felt wrong that there should be such a peaceful place given all that was going on.

"Hold." Darmin slowed and trotted over to a particular patch of grass.

Nothing about it looked remarkable to Danny, then he spotted a tiny speck of blue mixed in with the green. It was the most vivid, electric blue he'd ever seen. At least outside of a neon sign back home.

Darmin crouched and plucked two of the blue flowers before straightening and turning back to Danny. "This is good luck. Blue Blossom is very rare. I've never seen any in this part of the prairie."

"What's so special about them?" Danny asked.

Darmin held one of the flowers, which looked a bit like a wild rose, out to Danny. "They bring good health. We eat them whenever we find them."

"Good health, huh?" Sybil said beastfolk never got sick, so he couldn't imagine why they'd need to eat a flower.

Well, whatever. Maybe it was some cultural thing. Danny channeled ether through the blossom and confirmed it wasn't poisonous. Just to be on the safe side, he pulled a single petal and popped it in his mouth.

The bitterness made him gag and he spat it out, coughing. "That is nasty!"

"You don't like it?" Darmin sounded serious.

"No." Danny handed the flower back. "Here, you can have my share of the good health."

Darmin smiled and chomped down the second flower. "Thank you!"

Danny shook his head and they got back to running.

The rest of the journey was uneventful and as the sun dipped lower in the sky, the walls of Redfield appeared ahead of them. They really had made good time using Darmin's shortcut.

"This is where we part company, my friend," Darmin said. "I hope we meet again."

"Likewise." They did the odd arm wrestling handshake

before Darmin trotted back the way he'd come. Danny didn't bother mentioning that it would be every bit as dangerous for Darmin returning alone as it would've been for Danny to make the trip to Redfield alone. He was pretty sure Darmin had simply wanted to see him safely home as a way of saying thanks.

Putting the beastfolk out of his mind, Danny jogged the last couple miles to Redfield. When he was a little ways away he could see people shouting. There was a crowd gathered at the gate and the guards were holding them back while a priest tried to speak over the shouting crowd.

What the hell was going on now?

He activated his stealth field and snuck closer. He reached listening distance just as the people quieted enough for the priest to speak.

"No one can leave or enter," the priest said. "By order of the guilds and temples, Redfield is sealed until the plague has been stamped out. Return to your homes and keep calm. Sick people should make their way to the temple of the Goddess. We will do our best to help as many as we can."

Danny stopped listening. How had the plague made it into Redfield? And more importantly, how was Lise? He needed to get in and find out, quarantine be damned.

☾

The curved edge of Lise's kitchen knife sliced through the carrots with ease as she got ready to put them in the soup pot for lunch. The kitchen was warm from the oven and filled with the scent of baking bread and simmering broth. She'd only been working here for a day and Lise already found her spirits lifted. Having something real and useful to do did wonders to distract her.

At the counter beside her, the youngest of the inn's serving girls, a cute and lively thing who seemed unaware of the meaning of the word tired, worked alongside her, chattering about her brother's upcoming wedding as she peeled potatoes with little precision but great vigor.

"Careful," Lise said. "You don't want to nick your fingers."

"You sound like my mom. She's always nagging me to slow down. Be careful, Petra. Don't take off so much of the fruit with the peel, Petra. When are you getting married, Petra. I swear it's always something."

Being compared to Petra's mother was both a wonderful compliment and a painful one. It made her think of her own lost family. But it didn't make her cry and Lise considered that an improvement. Though it hadn't been long, she savored the easy camaraderie and sense of normality it brought. Traveling with Ronin was wonderful, but, kind as he was, he made a point a maintaining a certain distance and formality with her. Not that she had any right to complain after all he'd done.

When the time came, Lise was seriously thinking of settling in Redfield permanently. It felt a bit like home already.

The murmur of the late breakfast crowd filtered through the kitchen door. The bulk of the people had cleared out, but a few of the older folks liked to linger and chat. No one minded, even Emile the bartender tolerated them without complaint. Lise wouldn't have believed the grumpy man had a nice side, but when he wasn't rushing around and exhausted, he was a decent fellow.

Lise was just thinking how peaceful it was when a scream from the common room nearly cost her a finger.

"What was that?" Petra asked.

"Let's go see." Lise set her knife on the cutting board and pushed through the door.

The patrons as well as the other serving girls were standing in a circle around a coughing, twitching woman about ten years Lise's senior. No one seemed to know what to do as violent coughs and convulsions wracked the woman's body.

"I'll fetch a healer," Lise said. "Stay with her." That last bit was addressed to no one in particular and she didn't expect her request to be honored. No one wanted to get too close to someone showing any signs of illness right now.

Lise soon left the Golden Gate behind as she hurried through the busy streets. It was a good thing she'd gone to the Goddess's temple with Ronin the other day. She wouldn't have had a clue where to go otherwise.

No one troubled her on her way and soon she stood before the temple door. She ignored the stained glass window and pushed through without slowing. Father Sander, the same priest she'd met on her previous visit, waited in the chapel. Was someone always there on the off chance a person showed up looking for help?

Lise dismissed the question as irrelevant. "Please, a woman has fallen ill at the Golden Gate Inn."

Father Sander hurried over. "Tell me everything."

Lise did so, her voice faltering when she described the woman's symptoms. "You have to help her."

Father Sander wore a grave expression, his lips pressed into a thin line. He nodded once and shouted, "Father Oude, cover for me! Lead me to her, quickly."

Lise turned and hastened back the way she'd come. The city was a blur as they nearly ran through the streets. All Lise could think was that every second they delayed might cost that poor woman her life.

The front door of the inn swung open with a crash. Lise's breath came in gasps. She was in decent shape, but running wasn't really her thing. Father Sander appeared untroubled as he crossed the now nearly empty common room.

Only the victim, still coughing on the floorboards, and the staff, clustered near the bar watching like spectators at the horse races, remained. Emile had returned from the market while she was gone, and what a scene to return to.

Lise wasn't sure what to do, so she sort of hovered halfway between Father Sander and her co-workers.

For his part, the priest knelt beside the unfortunate woman, his hands glowing faintly above her shivering figure. His brow furrowed as he worked. Eventually the coughing slowed as the woman's breathing normalized.

"Father?" Lise asked.

"I've done all I can. She has the plague and I lack the power to heal it. All I managed was to ease her symptoms."

"How the hell did the plague get into the city?" Emile asked. "I thought you priests were checking everyone."

"We are, but, while we serve the archangels, we are not all knowing and all seeing. Everyone has done their best." He stood. "If you'll excuse me, I need to alert the other temples. I'll send bearers for her when I get back. We can look after her better at the temple. You'll need to remain inside for two days. If you show no symptoms by then, you're in the clear."

"What about the inn?" Emile asked.

"Closed, for two days. I'll reevaluate then. Bear in mind that if you leave, you risk contaminating your neighbors and anyone else you encounter. Do the right thing." With that unsettling pronouncement, Father Sander hurried away.

"'Do the right thing' he says," Emile snarled as Lise joined the others at the bar. "Easy for him to say. He doesn't have a business to run. What the hell are we supposed to do for two days?"

"What am I going to tell my mom?" Petra asked. "I can't go home and risk her getting sick."

"It's pointless anyway," Deb said. "All the customers have gone home already. They're probably spreading the plague everywhere they visit."

She had a point, but Lise didn't know what they could do about it. Despite her desire for a bit of independence, she dearly wished Ronin was here right now.

CHAPTER 14

Danny approached Redfield's gate, his stealth field making him both silent and invisible. The worst of the shouting had died down and the crowd was slowly breaking up as the people realized they had no hope of forcing their way through the armed guards. As for the guards, to a man they looked relieved that they wouldn't be forced to cut down their fellow citizens.

On the downside, they showed no sign of leaving the area around the gate. Trying to sneak in there was too risky despite his magic. On the plus side, Redfield's wall was no real barrier to him. Danny jogged about a hundred yards north, gathered himself, and leapt over the wall with ease. He landed on the grass behind the Goddess's temple and hurried around to the front.

People stood in a long line in front of the door. Coughs shook their bodies and some looked like they could barely stand. How had it gotten this bad so quickly? Danny had only been gone for two days and when he left no one was sick.

A quick look around the district confirmed similar lines at the other temples. There was no way the priests would be able to handle this many people. In fact, he doubted there were any priests capable of healing the plague in Redfield. From what he'd seen, only an especially powerful priest had any hope of curing it.

Danny hurried away. He needed to check on Lise, but first a quick side trip. Silent strides carried him to the marketplace. The stalls and shops were quiet, but there was one person doing a booming business.

Osbern's wagon was surrounded by well-dressed people while a larger group of the less-well-off formed a ring around them. Danny had seen aid trucks end up surrounded like this and it could get ugly in a hurry.

Looked like the guards knew it too. Three men in leather armor stood ready, their swords bare in their hands. Danny frowned. Three? There had only been two guards when Danny spoke with Osbern the first time. Where had he found a new guard in Redfield? Maybe he was an adventurer. Guard duty in exchange for a cure potion would be a pretty sweet deal.

"Step right up! A cure for the plague awaits! One vial and you'll be as good as new." If his smile was any indication, Osbern was in his glory. How anyone could be remotely happy surrounded by so much misery was another question.

Something weird was definitely going on with the merchant, but Danny would have to sort it out later. With a final glare at the potion seller and his hired swords, Danny slipped away. Hopefully Lise would be able to tell him something about what had happened after he left.

The silent streets were creepy as Danny quickened his pace toward the Golden Gate Inn. It was nearly dark and the evening air had a bite to it along with a hint of moisture. He wouldn't be surprised to see snow by morning. One more bit of misery heaped on the already unfortunate people of Redfield.

Danny paused outside the entrance and cast a silence spell over the door. He didn't want anyone to notice his arrival. A quick tug confirmed that the door was locked. Hardly a surprise under the circumstances. Focusing on the ether, Danny formed a tiny hand and used it to slide the bolt open. As soon as he was inside he locked the door behind him.

The common room was empty. The bartender and serving girls had either gone home or hunkered down in an empty room. He'd worry about them later. Taking the stairs two at a time, Danny rushed up to his room. Pausing outside to collect himself, he pushed the door open.

As he feared, Lise was in bed, shivering and wheezing. Danny ended his stealth field and closed the door.

She looked up at him as he approached the bed. Lise opened her mouth to say something but only a wracking cough emerged.

"Easy, Lise. This will only take a moment." Danny drew ether through her body and charged it with holy energy. As with the villagers in White Hall, he infused every cell of her body, purging the disease in the process. It took a good deal less energy this time, no doubt because she hadn't been sick as long as the villagers.

When her breathing grew steady he ended the spell. "Better?"

Lise nodded, tears in the corners of her eyes. "I thought I was going to die and was surprised the idea troubled me. Thank you, Ronin."

"I'm glad I got back in time. What happened?"

"I started working in the kitchen," Lise said. "It was nice. Everyone treated me well, even Emile."

"Emile?" Danny asked.

"The bartender. That's his name. You wouldn't think it, but he's a bit of a softie under that gruff exterior. Anyway, at breakfast this morning, one of the patrons collapsed in a coughing fit. I went to find Father Sander and by the time I got back all the other customers had left, no doubt spreading the disease to everyone they met. By noon we were all coughing. What time is it anyway?"

"Sunset. You've been sick for about six hours." Danny shook his head. "Six hours. How could so many people be so sick in such a short time? It doesn't make sense. The process should've taken days at least and more likely weeks."

He was mostly talking to himself so it was a surprise when Lise spoke. "Can you heal the others too?"

"Of course. They're my next stop. What I can't do is heal the entire town, more's the pity. Once you're all better, I'm going to need you to stay inside and away from everyone else. My magic only cures the disease, it grants no long-term immunity."

"I understand. Thank you."

Danny squeezed her hand and slipped out of their room. He could sense the others' life forces and, following his magical awareness, went from room to room purging the disease from first the serving girls then the bartender. There were no guests, which he assumed was because the other people lodging here had gone out and not been able to return after the outbreak.

Whatever the case, using so much magic combined with a long day of running had left Danny exhausted. Since he couldn't do anything more tonight anyway, he returned to his room. Lise was sound asleep, her breathing steady and normal with no hint of a wheeze. Looked like he'd gotten all the virus cells out of her.

Good. He just wished he could do the same for the rest of the people.

What he could do was find whoever was responsible for this and make sure they didn't do it anywhere else.

CHAPTER 15

Danny pulled his worn leather boots on. He didn't know how many miles he'd put on them, but suspected it was a lot. The world might be technologically primitive compared to Earth, but they had a knack for making sturdy clothes. Beside him Lise snored away. Her thankfully brief illness had left her worn out. Not wanting to bother her, Danny slipped silently out of their room.

He descended the wooden staircase to the inn's common room. Hopefully they had enough food on hand for him to fix breakfast. He hadn't eaten anything but wolf meat and jerky for two days and he was starving.

Danny paused at the bottom of the steps. To his considerable surprise, Emile the bartender as well as all three serving girls were awake and sitting around a table near the bar. They all stared at him as he approached.

"Morning," Danny said. "How are you all feeling?"

"Better," Emile said. "When I went to bed last night, I doubted I'd see the morning. Instead I wake up fully recovered and a man I know wasn't in the city yesterday is here. I hardly think that's a coincidence."

"It's not. I healed you all last night. Fortunately you hadn't been sick for that long so it didn't take too much out of me. And all I did was restore you. The magic offers no immunity, so you can get infected again should you have the bad luck to run into someone sick."

"We'll be sticking to the inn until the priests give the all clear." Emile gave him a narrow-eyed look. "How did you get back in anyway? There was an announcement that the town would be sealed until the outbreak ran its course."

"There are very few places that can keep me out should I wish to get in. Redfield isn't one of them. I turned invisible then jumped over the wall with no one the wiser." Danny grinned. "Would you have preferred I stayed out?"

"Hell no. I was just curious." Emile pushed himself to his feet. "I'll handle breakfast and from now on your room is on the house."

"Thanks." Danny sat in the chair Emile had vacated.

He'd barely settled in when the girls all leaned toward him with big smiles and low-cut tops. It was a pretty sight, no question.

"We'd like to thank you too," one of them said as she ran her hand along his arm.

Danny grinned again then caught himself. He really needed to sort the contraception thing out.

"Easy now." Fun as it would've been, Danny didn't want to do anything that might lead to a misunderstanding. Technically, he would've happily done something that might lead to a misunderstanding, but he had more self-control than someone his age normally would've.

"Did I miss anything interesting?" Danny turned to see Lise standing at the bottom of the stairs, arms crossed.

The girls hopped to their feet and scattered like bunnies before a fox. Their reaction amused Danny so much that he didn't get mad. In fact, it was a bit of a relief.

"How're you feeling?" Danny asked.

"Better than yesterday, though apparently not as good as you." Lise's reply was a bit sharp.

"The girls were just showing their gratitude. Not that it's any of your concern." Danny winced as soon as he said it. Still, it wasn't like Lise was his wife or girlfriend or anything. She had no claim on him.

"You're right, sorry. I've had you to myself for so long I felt a bit jealous seeing three pretty girls half my age paying attention to you. Silly, I know, since you've made it clear where we stand. Just friends, I remember."

Emile emerged from the kitchen carrying a platter covered with sausages, fried eggs, and perfectly golden toast. Danny's mouth watered at the sight of it. He took a laden plate and a mug of watered wine and dug in.

Happily no one felt the need to talk and far too soon the meal concluded. "I'm heading to the Adventurers' Guild. I picked up a few clues during my visit with the beastfolk and I'm hoping they can fill in some blanks. Remember, don't let anyone else in."

"As if we needed the reminder," Emile said. "I doubt anyone will be out and about in any case."

Danny couldn't argue with his assessment. He pushed back his chair, stood, and headed for the door, grabbing his cloak from a hook on his way. And it was well that he did. Outside, the air was bitter cold and the streets empty. At least it hadn't snowed; that was a small blessing, one that couldn't last.

He debated activating his stealth field but doubted anyone would trouble him. In fact, no one even poked their head out to speak with him and soon he stood in front of the Adventurers' Guild. Whether or not he could get any help here was another matter, but if he couldn't, Danny figured his next move would be to have a word with Osbern, the suddenly popular potion merchant. That guy had to know more than he said last time they spoke.

Danny had ways of making people talk.

Danny paused outside the guild and listened. Adventurers were usually a rowdy bunch, which made the complete silence even more unnerving, though it was also in complete keeping with the rest of Redfield. He hadn't seen a soul on his way here. Danny couldn't help wondering how many people were in their homes, dying by inches.

He shook the thought away. Best not to think about it.

The door rattled but refused to open when he pushed on it. That wasn't a great sign. The guild was usually open all day every day.

A little telekinetic magic worked the bolt loose and Danny slipped into the empty waiting room. The interior was dim, not that there was anything to see besides empty tables and an unoccupied counter.

He closed the door and crossed the room to the counter. Peeking over it, he let out a breath of relief. No bodies, thank heaven.

"Hello?" No reply of course. He hadn't really expected one. Much like at the inn, he figured everyone was laid up.

Opening himself fully to the ether, Danny sensed three life forces, one on the first floor and two above. Assuming this guild was set up the same as the one in Rosenbar, the downstairs one was likely the guild master in his office. That struck him as a good place to start, so Danny set out down the hall. It was creepy as hell in the empty, silent building and every moment Danny expected someone to jump out and yell, "Boo!"

No one did of course and soon he paused at the guild master's door. The muffled sounds of heavy coughs came through, confirming his fears. Danny pushed the door open and found a man, the guild master he assumed, slumped over his desk. His skin was pallid and sweat beaded on his brow. He looked at Danny as if seeing a ghost.

"Guild Master?" Danny asked.

He tried to answer but more coughs cut him off.

Right, healing first, questions later.

Danny channeled ether infused with holy energy through the guild master's body. It took a bit longer than when he healed Lise, but eventually the disease was burned away. Danny wasn't sure if he was getting better at healing or if the plague had mutated into something less severe. Either way he was happy with the results.

"Who are you?" the guild master asked, his voice rough from all the coughing. "Not one of the regulars."

"No, sir. I'm Ronin. I only arrived in Redfield a couple days ago. How are you feeling?"

"Better. Thank you. Are you a priest?"

"No, sir, an arcane knight. My healing magic works a bit

differently than the priests' but it is effective. Are the secretaries upstairs?"

"Yes. I didn't want to send them home as sick as they were. They'd never forgive themselves if they made their families ill as well. Would you...?"

"Yup. Rest a bit. I'll be back shortly and we can exchange notes."

Danny left the office and retraced his steps to the staircase. At the top he followed his magical senses to a room at the back. He pushed open the door to the secretaries' room. The two women were somewhere between asleep and delirious as they tossed and turned on sweat-soaked sheets. Their breath was shallow and wheezy, their faces pale and drawn tight with pain. They looked worse than the guild master.

Danny repeated the healing process and sure enough these two took longer to purify. But he did succeed in curing them and that was all that mattered. As soon as he ended the spell, they fell into a calm, deep sleep. Satisfied, Danny stepped back into the hall.

With the secretaries on the mend, Danny went back to the first floor. He found the guild master sitting up straighter in his chair, his eyes clear and alert. That was a good sign.

"How are the girls?" the guild master asked.

"Sleeping and on the mend. They'll be weak for a day or two, but they should make a full recovery. I have to warn you that my magic only cures the disease, it doesn't offer immunity."

"Noted," the guild master said. "Name's Reggie and I'm most grateful for what you did."

"I'm glad I could help. If I had the power, I'd heal everyone in town, but I can only help a few people each day.

If I overdo it, I'll be too weak to do anything else. Can you tell me what happened?"

"People started getting sick yesterday morning. It happened suddenly. Redfield went from having no sick people to a full-on epidemic overnight. Magic must've been involved, though how, I can't begin to guess. As soon as we started to feel ill, I locked up the guild. How did you get in anyway?"

"Magic. Where are the rest of the adventurers?"

"Either out of town on jobs or at their inns. Like I said, my only interest was in keeping them away from the guild so they didn't end up sick. Though the way things are looking now, I was probably wasting my time."

"You tried to do the right thing and that's not nothing. If I wanted to find out who entered Redfield in the… let's say six hours before the first person got sick, who would I talk to?"

"No one. Far as I'm aware, no one keeps track of who comes and goes. As long as you pay your entry fee and aren't sick, you can enter."

"That's not terribly convenient." Reggie let out a huge yawn, drawing a faint smile from Danny. "You'd best lie down and get some sleep."

"What are you going to do?" Reggie asked.

"I'm going to have a chat with Osbern the potion merchant. His business went from lousy to booming in a day and when I saw him both he and his guards were in perfect health despite being surrounded by people sick with the most aggressive plague I've ever seen. He's hiding something and I mean to find out what."

CHAPTER 16

Danny left the Adventurers' Guild behind and made his way toward the market. He was relieved the staff would recover. Whether Redfield as a whole recovered was another matter altogether. He hoped it did, but as things stood now he wasn't optimistic.

As he walked, a strange thought crossed his mind. He hadn't seen a single town guard on patrol. Some of them should've been out if only to make sure people knew to stay inside until the crisis was over. On the plus side it saved him the trouble of using his stealth field to avoid them.

The journey was a brief one and soon he was passing empty, unmanned stalls. He didn't know what the town's food situation was, but with winter nearly upon them, Danny assumed they had their supplies laid in. The timing of the outbreak might end up a blessing in disguise.

He paused when the thud of steps caught his attention. A moment later, a lone man came running around the bend, a bright-blue potion clutched in his hands. He shot a furtive look at Danny before shifting his body to block his view of the potion and running on.

Putting the nervous fellow out of his mind, Danny focused on Osbern's wagon. No crowd surrounded it today. His first thought was that they were out of product, but the desperate man from a second ago disproved that theory. Well, whatever. He'd find out eventually.

All three guards were on duty with the new guy in the center of a small arc in front of the wagon. Osbern was absent at the moment, but Danny assumed the merchant was in the back of his wagon. As he got closer, one of the original guards leaned in and whispered to the new one. The man's sullen expression grew harder.

"Show your gold or shove off," the new guard said. "We've had enough of beggars."

"Osbern around?" Danny asked, more to gauge their reaction than out of any real curiosity about the chubby merchant's whereabouts.

"What part of 'show your gold or shove off' did you misunderstand?" the guard asked.

"Would Captain Koch approve of your attitude?" Danny asked.

The youngest guard, a man not much older than Danny's host body, asked, "How do you know the captain?"

"A fellow by the name of Peter mentioned him to me," Danny said. "An acquaintance of yours I believe. Or perhaps comrade in arms would be more appropriate."

The new guard drew his sword. "Osbern said you were trouble. Looks like he got something right for a change. You should know better than to stick your nose where it doesn't belong, kid."

Danny grinned. He'd fought demons, ogres, and a fire drake—these idiots were nuisances in comparison. An effort of will wrapped all three of them in ethereal chains. Once they were safely bound Danny took their swords as well as a collection of daggers before stepping around to the rear of the wagon.

A heavy canvas flap covered the back and Danny yanked it aside. Osbern cowered inside surrounded by crates, a hefty bag of coins sitting in his lap. He stared at Danny, eyes wide with fear.

"Time for another chat, Osbern," Danny said. "This time you're going to tell me everything."

"You can't just do whatever you want," Osbern sputtered, his voice a pitiful mix of defiance and dread. "There are laws."

Danny looked left and right at the empty market. "Who's going to stop me? Not your pitiful excuse for guards, that's for sure. No, you're going to talk to me, Osbern. Either willingly or with a bit of coaxing. Either way works for me, though I admit I wouldn't mind a bit of coaxing."

Danny offered his best evil smile. The threat hung heavy between them. Osbern whimpered. A more pathetic sound Danny had never heard.

At last Osbern said, "I didn't have anything to do with the plague, you understand. The only part I played was selling the cure. You might even say I'm a hero."

"You're a lot of things, Osbern, but that sure as hell isn't one of them. Now, who gave you the potions?"

"I don't know his name." Danny raised a fist. "It's the truth, I swear. I was one of three merchants chosen to distribute the cure. I came east, another went west and a final south. I don't think you fully appreciate just how big this project is. My master's plans extend far beyond this miserable little chunk of the world. Not that he shared the details with the likes of me. I had my task and it was made clear that I didn't need to worry about anything else. I was happy to comply. If you'd met my master, you would've been as well."

"I fully intend to introduce myself to the son of a bitch as soon as possible. He's set up at an old elf-blood outpost, right?"

Osbern nodded. "I'm impressed you know about that as well. It seems you've been busy. Yes, the outpost is his base. The beastfolk slaves work the fields nearby growing the ingredients necessary to create the cure."

He laid it out so calmly, as if real people weren't dying every day just so he could make some coin. Danny's disgust must have shown on his face.

"I didn't lift a finger against anyone, myself," Osbern said, his mustache quivering with each word. "Does that count for nothing? If I hadn't agreed to distribute the cure, someone else would've done it."

"Keep telling yourself that if it makes you feel better. For myself, I think nothing less than beating you half to death will make me feel better."

"No!" Osbern scrambled back, tossed crates aside, and ripped open a hidden panel. He pulled a crystal ball out of the nook, his pudgy hands trembling. "Here, take it. You can use this to speak to my master yourself."

"I knew you were holding out on me." Danny snatched the orb. "You're going to take what's left of your potions to the temple of the Goddess. Every potion, every coin, all of it goes to those in need."

Osbern's mouth opened, but before he could speak Danny said, "I'm not making a request, Osbern. I'll be coming along to make sure it's done properly."

A nod, meek and resigned, was all Osbern could muster. Good. Hopefully the potions would turn the tide.

◌

D anny sat beside Osbern on the wagon bench as they made their way through the silent streets of Redfield. It had come as a pleasant surprise when Danny learned Osbern knew how to both hitch up the horses and drive the wagon himself. The merchant held himself somewhat stiffer than a board as he grasped the reins. No doubt Danny's dagger in his ribs had something to do with it.

Technically the weapon wasn't necessary. Danny could've killed the greedy pig with a thought, but there was something clarifying to the mind about having a foot of razor-sharp steel a couple of inches from your flesh. Suffice it to say, Osbern was on his best behavior. In the back of the wagon, the three mercenaries lay bound and silent, surrounded by crates of potions.

It didn't take long to make the trip back across town to the temple district. A line of fifteen people waited outside the Goddess's temple, so Danny had Osbern park on a side street out of sight. As soon as the brake was thrown Danny bound the merchant with ethereal chains and threw him in the back of the wagon with his goons.

"I'll be back in a minute, don't go anywhere." Osbern threw Danny a silent glare which made him grin. The piece of shit's suffering pleased Danny no end.

Leaving the wagon, Danny hurried around to the front of the temple. He skirted the line of fifteen or so of the saddest-looking people he'd seen in a long time. None of them even had the strength to complain as he slipped through the front door. Danny hated cutting the line, but it wasn't like he was going to take anyone's bed.

A quick glance into the chapel confirmed that Father Sander wasn't there. It also confirmed that every square foot was occupied by coughing, wheezing patients forced to lie on the floor.

With a little shake of his head, Danny headed for the infirmary. The room, about three times the size of the chapel, was also packed with the sick and the dying. Father Sander stood beside the bed of a boy who couldn't have been older than six. The priest's hands glowed with divine energy as he channeled the archangel's power. The kid's breathing eased and a bit of color returned to his cheeks. He was far from cured, but it looked like the crisis had passed for the moment.

When the priest straightened, Danny called out, "Father Sander? Do you have a moment?"

"Ronin." Father Sander shuffled his way, looking nearer to eighty than forty. Clearly the work was taking its toll. "Are you feeling ill?"

"No, Father, I'm fine. I have some semi-good news. There's a partial wagonload of cure potions on the side street ready for you to distribute."

"It's against the law for you to steal them regardless of how badly they're needed."

"I didn't steal them, I prevailed upon Osbern's good nature. It wasn't hard to convince him once I learned he was working for the guy that set the plague loose on the world."

Father Sander's brow furrowed. "I'm not sure I understand. Someone started the plague? How? Why? To sell potions and get rich? What good is wealth if everyone's dead?"

Danny filled him in on everything he'd learned. "The how and the why are still a bit vague, but tracking down Osbern's master is the next thing on my to-do list. Anyway, I've got four prisoners and nowhere to put them. I was told the Merchants' Guild and the temples were in charge of Redfield, so I figured you could tell me where to take them."

"Goddess be merciful," Father Sander said. "That might be the worst story I've ever heard. Such vile actions. I don't even know where to begin."

"I say we begin by giving out those potions to the sickest people first. I have the prisoners bound with magic, but I can't maintain the spell forever."

"Of course. Forgive me, I was a bit shocked by everything." Father Sander turned away from Danny and said, "Michael, join us please."

One of the two younger priests set the bucket he'd been carrying down and jogged over. He was nearly as haggard as his superior, with his white robe stained with sweat and sticking to his skin. "Father?"

"Come along." Father Sander led the group out of the temple and down the street to where Danny had left the wagon. "I want you to handle the distribution of these potions, starting with those closest to death. I'll be along shortly."

Michael climbed up on the wagon bench while Danny dragged his prisoners out the back. They landed in the street with meaty thuds. That done, Michael urged the horses forward.

"Follow me," Father Sander said. "Branik's temple also serves as the town's jail and courthouse."

Danny adjusted the binding spell to allow the men to walk then jerked them to their feet. "You heard the man, march!"

The mercenaries glared at Danny while Osbern settled for a whimper. When he reached for his sword the group started moving. Happily, Branik's temple was less than a block away. The plain, gray stone building had little in the way of charm. In fact, it would've looked right at home in the Dragon Empire back on Earth.

Father Sander knocked on the heavy wooden door and it soon opened. A young man with broad shoulders and wearing mail with a white tabard featuring an inverted sword bowed to Father Sander.

"Is Joris available?" Father Sander asked.

"Yes, Father." The young man looked around then in a low voice added, "He has failed to heal a single victim and it has left him despondent. If you can do anything to lift his mood, we would all be most grateful."

"I fear my news will do nothing to improve his mood. Would you get him, please?"

The young man bowed. "Excuse me, Father."

When he'd disappeared into the temple, Father Sander said, "Branik's followers aren't the most skilled at healing and this disease is the most magic resistant I've ever seen. Joris shouldn't be so hard on himself."

"Knowing that in your head and convincing your heart are two different things, Father," Danny said.

"Heaven knows that's true. I've seldom felt as inadequate as I have the last couple of days."

The temple door opened again, revealing an older version of the fellow that greeted them. He had the same outfit, same burly build, and a gray beard and bald head. "Father Sander, what brings you by?"

"Trouble, Joris. Can I tell you on the way to the cells?"

Joris favored Danny with a penetrating look before shifting his gaze to the bound mercenaries. "Certainly. Follow me."

The high priest led them down an undecorated stone hall. As they walked, Father Sander repeated everything Danny had told him. Danny could see the tension building as Joris's stride grew stiffer and the muscles in his neck bunched.

Soon enough they reached a room with three iron-barred cells. Joris unlocked two of them and Danny shoved the mercenaries into one and Osbern into the other. As soon as the doors were locked he ended the binding spell.

Leaving the jail behind, they emerged into the hall. "I can't believe anyone would release such a disease on purpose," Joris said.

"Believe it," Danny said. "The question now is, what can the temples do to help put an end to the one responsible?"

Father Sander sighed. "Our temples have no influence beyond Redfield, Ronin. The wilderness obeys no law but power."

"That might be for the best," Danny said. "I can do what I have to without worrying about corrupt officials or bribed guards."

"I wish I could do more than wish you luck." Father Sander extended a hand and Danny shook it. "Redfield owes you more than we can ever repay."

"Thanks, Father. I'll be back as soon as I can, hopefully

with good news." Danny left the temple and headed for the Golden Gate Inn. He'd say goodbye to Lise before swinging by the guild to, if luck was with him, find a map that led to the elves' outpost. Once that was done, he'd be on the road once more.

CHAPTER 17

The Western Trade Road stretched through the grasslands for as far as Danny could see. He'd succeeded in finding a map of the area at the Adventurers' Guild. It wasn't as detailed as he would've liked, but it was better than the one in the elvish gazetteer. That one didn't even show the outpost he was looking for. That argued the location wasn't important to the elves.

Danny was quite curious to see what it looked like. Back on Earth, elf ruins were considered death traps that no sane person visited willingly. Hopefully the ones on Valindor wouldn't be as bad. Dealing with a crazy, evil wizard would be trouble enough.

He'd said goodbye to Lise two days ago. She hadn't even made a fuss, which he appreciated. Danny was optimistic that she would be content to settle in Redfield permanently, freeing him to continue his mission at a faster clip. Assuming he could sort out this plague business. At the very least killing the one responsible for starting it should help.

Despite the clear, beautiful weather, Danny hadn't seen a

single merchant since leaving Redfield. Hopefully that meant they were being careful as opposed to being dead. All things considered, he figured the latter was more likely.

He paused and pulled out his new map. There wasn't much around here. The next village was off a side road another twenty miles ahead. Danny planned to keep his distance. Much as he wanted to help as many people as he could, he needed to keep moving.

Before he could resume his journey, Danny sensed three potent, inhuman life forces headed rapidly his way. Thankfully there was no corruption, which meant they weren't demons. A moment later he spotted them, three of the new giant Alpha Wolves charging right at him.

Of all the rotten luck. Danny pulled the ethersword out of storage and lit it. He drew ether into his body, making his muscles stronger and his bones as hard as steel.

The first wolf leapt at him far too quickly for something so big.

Of course, fast was a relative thing. Compared to the demon king, the wolves were barely moving. Danny dodged it with feet to spare. A hard slash of the ethersword removed the beast's head.

Trying to take advantage of the death of their pack mate, the other two attacked from opposite sides.

Danny threw his hands out, hurling a telekinetic blast in all directions.

The spell picked the wolves up and hurled them twenty yards through the air.

Danny charged right, slicing through the second wolf's lower jaw when it tried to bite him. A quick thrust through the chest finished it.

He spun just in time to get tackled by half a ton of leaping wolf.

His back hit the ground and Danny kicked hard with both legs, sending the beast flying. Before it reached the ground, he hit it with a full power blast of lightning strengthened by the ethersword's mithril hilt.

The force of the blast turned the wolf into a crimson mist.

When nothing else attacked him for ten seconds, Danny deactivated the ethersword and returned it to his storage.

They were tougher than crimson ogres for sure. He hated to think about some poor beastfolk hunters having to fight those things. Without magic backing them up, he could well imagine the losses they'd face.

He was about to resume his journey when a vibration from his satchel brought him up short. What the hell was that?

Rummaging around, he soon found the source. The vibrations were coming from the crystal ball Danny got from Osbern. He pulled it out and it began to glow. The light soon resolved into a face, its features gaunt and twisted. Danny had seldom seen a face that screamed "evil wizard" more perfectly than this one.

"You must be the adventurer Osbern mentioned. If you have his crystal ball may I assume he and his guards are dead?"

"You can assume whatever you like. Are you the lunatic behind this plague?"

"Behind it?" The wizard's confusion seemed genuine. "The plague is perfectly natural, leaving aside a modest alteration to make it less susceptible to priestly healing. It's been around since the time of the elves, not that they were ever troubled by anything so ordinary as a disease."

"If you're claiming you did nothing to spread it then I say you're full of shit."

"What a charming expression. We let it spread by introducing it to the beastfolk who, with their natural immunity, made perfect carriers. We also provided a cure."

"For a price."

"All things have a price. But enough of this pointless chatter. You killed three of my Ultra Wolves, which makes you exceptionally skilled. What will it take for you to come to our side? I have considerable resources at my disposal."

"I can't think of anything. My only goal is to end this before any more people die. My hope is that your death will help."

"You're an adventurer, are you not?" the wizard asked. "I'm offering to hire you. I'll even make it official at the Discourt guild."

"I've already been hired by the mayor of White Hall to end the plague."

"That is unfortunate. It seems we have nothing more to discuss."

Ether surged through the orb.

Danny hurled it away with all his might. The explosion that filled the air looked like the brightest fireworks ever. He never had any intention of letting the wizard escape, but now it seemed war had been officially declared.

○

Danny strode down a rough dirt track, his cloak pulled tight against the chill. He'd been trying to avoid using any more magic than necessary just in case this guy ended up being tough enough to cause him trouble. The odds of that weren't great, but better to assume the worst and be pleasantly surprised.

He'd left the Western Trade Road behind a day ago and now, at least according to his map, he was about half a day away from the outpost. The area was hilly, with lots of low undulations that made it hard to see farther than a quarter of a mile or so. Having gotten used to the open plains, it felt claustrophobic. Even more strange was the lack of opposition. Since the Ultra Wolf attack, Danny hadn't seen anyone or anything more threatening than a herd of antelope. His luck, he feared, would change far sooner than he would've liked.

An hour later his prediction came true. At the top of a little rise he spotted a group of ten armed figures marching down the path. They wore leather armor and carried a mix of spears and swords. One had a strung bow with a quiver of arrows at his hip. More mercenaries. Better than giant wolves, but still a nuisance. Taking them out wouldn't be a problem. One well-placed fireball would do the trick.

It would also reveal his presence as clearly as a lit torch on a moonless night. Danny preferred not to lose the element of surprise just yet.

Activating his stealth field, he left the path behind and worked his way around the scrub-dotted knolls, making a path around the patrol. Invisible and silent though he might be, he still bent blades of grass as he passed. If anyone was paying attention, they'd be bound to notice if he got too close.

Half a mile later he returned to the road and picked up his pace. Danny wanted to reach the outpost well before dark. Scouting in daylight was much easier than doing it at night.

He covered another five miles or so, evading a second patrol in the process. The terrain grew rougher by the stride. Finally he spotted the outpost.

At the top of the tallest hill, a rectangular, moss-covered building rose out of the grass. It looked like someone had gone to a bit of trouble trying to camouflage it, but in the end it was so unnatural sitting where it did that trying to make it look like part of nature was a waste of time. The outpost had neither a door nor windows. At least it had none on this side. He'd make a full survey in a moment. For now, there was another area that caught his eye.

Danny's gaze shifted to a sprawling field at the base of the hill. Neat rows of bright-blue flowers swayed in an unnaturally warm breeze. He recognized the Blue Blossoms immediately. What he couldn't figure out was how so many of them were growing so big and so well in this cold. The one Darmin showed him was a little, kind of shriveled thing which, despite its vibrant color, looked like it had been hit by a frost.

Even from this distance he could make out the stocky, fur-covered figures of two dozen beastfolk. That didn't seem like enough given how many packs Rafe said had gone missing.

One of them turned and a faint glow at the base of his neck caught Danny's eye. Using magic to sharpen his vision, he examined the strange mark. It was a spell circle, extremely complex despite its modest size. Danny didn't recognize the magic's function but suspected it had something to do with the slack and vacant expressions on their faces. Psychic magic of some sort was his guess.

Much as he wanted to help, Danny forced himself to hang back. Even if he freed them, he had nowhere to take them and the last thing he needed was for them to get mixed up in the fight he knew was coming.

First he'd deal with the wizard, then he'd free the slaves.

Those marks weren't the only magic here. Ether glowed throughout the soil. That had to be the cause of both the unnatural warmth and the Blue Blossoms' excessive growth. As with the spell circle, his host body had no knowledge of such magic or its source.

There were too many mysteries here for his liking. Unraveling them seemed to be his destiny in life. For now, he needed to figure out how to get inside the outpost.

Leaving the unfortunate beastfolk to their work, Danny made a full circle around the building. And found exactly nothing. There was nothing to distinguish one side from the next. They were all just as free from doors and windows and all just as covered with moss.

Since there was no housing outside the outpost, he assumed the slaves were brought in at some point. He'd have to wait until someone came out to get them. Once the door was down, getting in would be simple.

In theory at least. Only time would tell if he'd guessed right.

So he sat on the ground about a hundred yards from the side of the outpost facing the beastfolk and settled in to wait. His stealth field would ensure no one noticed him. Assuming the wizard himself didn't come out to collect his workers, and even then, unless he was looking for someone invisible, the odds were against anyone spotting him.

Sitting and waiting reminded Danny of some of the ops he'd carried out back on Earth. One time he and his team had surveilled a two-room stone hut for three days waiting for a terrorist leader to show up. When the asshole and his crew rolled up, all Danny had to do was point the designator at them and boom, hellfire enema from five thousand feet. Boring as it had been, at least none of his guys had been hurt. Those were the missions Danny liked best.

His reminiscing was cut short when a line of white light outlined a rectangle in the center of the outpost's blank wall. A moment later the door sank into the ground and a squad of leather-armored mercenaries emerged. They carried wooden truncheons and showed no signs of concern as they marched toward the beastfolk. The lead mercenary had a stone cylinder that glowed in the ether. A thread connected the cylinder to the now-lowered door. It had to serve as a key.

This was his chance. Danny sprinted toward the open door and slipped inside. It looked like the walls were made of steel rather than stone. Weird, but whatever. He darted right, making his way down the hall. He sensed a number of life forces scattered around the building, some on this level, some below, and some above. The wizard could be with any of them.

Looked like Danny was going to have to clear the entire structure. To be on the safe side, he took the ethersword out of storage. Unless his opponent had an enchanted weapon or armor, the ethersword would slice right through them. It felt like cheating, but in the end this was war and the only thing that mattered was winning.

At least the doors were visible inside the outpost. They each had a glowing rune beside them that he assumed you touched to open them. The first one he reached had no signs of life behind it so Danny touched the rune. The door slid down out of sight revealing a storeroom full of farm implements.

Not a terribly interesting discovery, but at least he knew for sure how the doors worked now.

He continued on until he reached a door with a number of life forces behind it. They were strong but didn't feel human. A tap of the rune sent the door out of sight. Danny stepped into a lab that featured four huge cages, each with a gray-furred puppy inside. The cute little guys growled at him when he got close, ears folded back and ready to fight. They looked healthy and well cared for. Whatever experiments they'd endured didn't appear to have done them any harm.

Danny wasn't sure how to react to the relatively good treatment of the puppies when compared with the treatment of the beastfolk. He liked puppies as much as the next person but they weren't people like the beastfolk.

He couldn't do anything for the pups at the moment so Danny returned to the hall to resume his hunt. He stalked through the winding corridors, expecting at any moment to run into a patrol of soldiers and finding nothing.

About three-quarters of the way through his search he found a set of stairs leading to the second floor. The odds said the wizard was up there. His training said you didn't move on until you finished clearing the entire floor. The odds won out and Danny started up the stairs.

At the top, he stepped into a single huge room. In the center was a spell circle about twenty feet in diameter. A figure wearing a black robe stood behind it facing Danny. A huge Ultra Wolf towered beside him. The light from the glowing circle cast weird shadows over the wizard's face, making him seem less than human.

"You made better time than I expected."

"You're remarkably calm, considering." Danny lit the ethersword. "I don't suppose I can convince you to surrender and tell me everything you know?"

"My master would be most displeased by that."

Danny frowned. "Master? I thought you were the top man."

The wizard laughed. "Hardly. I am a child compared to my master. He'll change the world. I'm content with improving the Alpha Wolves, for the moment at least."

"I'm not sure making them bigger and more aggressive is much of an improvement." Danny moved closer, working his way around the spell circle.

"It is if you want to create the ultimate predator. That's my goal."

"What's your master's goal?"

"To improve humanity. Personally, I think the world would be better off if we just wiped them all out, but then I lack his vision."

"I can think of a few humans in need of eliminating. Starting with you."

The thud of feet behind Danny brought an end to the conversation. Twenty mercenaries rushed into the room, swords drawn and bows at the ready.

"You were saying something about surrendering?" the wizard said. "I now make you the same offer. You can work the fields with the beastfolk. Not an overly pleasant fate, but at least you'll be alive."

"I'm going to have to pass."

"So I assumed. Kill him!"

The mercenaries attacked from one direction while the Ultra Wolf leapt right across the spell circle at him, fangs at the ready. It would've been a problem for anyone else.

Danny sent an explosion of ether surging out in every direction. Mercenaries scattered like tenpins. The giant wolf staggered but didn't fall. A single stride followed by an overhand swing separated its head from its neck.

A lightning bolt hammered into Danny's personal shield, staggering him back. The wizard approached, hands raised and ether crackling around his fingers.

"I hadn't expected such an impressive display." Another blast slammed into Danny, sending him flying across the room. "I thought you nothing but another overconfident adventurer."

Danny strengthened his shield and pretended to struggle to his feet. Maybe he could get something useful out of this guy by playing possum. "And yet I still managed to deal with your merchant and his guards and make it here. What does it say about you and your master that a mere adventurer could do all that?"

A telekinetic blast hit Danny, throwing him back into the wall. "It says you got lucky. Do you think that idiot Osbern and three halfwit thugs will be difficult to replace? The loss of the potions will cost us a bit of revenue, but that's nothing in the grand scheme of things."

"I'm sure your master will be disappointed all the same." Danny got to his hands and knees. "Maybe you're the one that's going to end up replaced."

"He would never. Master Avius plucked me out of obscurity in the Discourt Magic Academy based solely on my overwhelming potential. I've been with him since nearly the beginning of his great task."

The name meant nothing to Danny, but that, along with the name of the magic academy, should provide him with enough information to get started tracking the head man. Off to the side, the mercenaries were starting to recover from his spell. Looked like it was time to wrap this up.

Danny shrugged off another lightning bolt and stood.

"I'm impressed you have strength enough to stand after all that. Truly it's well that I end you here. With a little more experience, you might have been a threat."

Ether gathered around the wizard as he prepared another spell.

Danny surged ether into his body and kicked the ground hard, leaping forward and closing the gap between them in an instant. The wizard's stunned expression as the ether-sword slid into his chest might have been amusing under other circumstances.

"May I have your name before you die?" Danny asked.

Instead of answering, a blood bubble rose from the wizard's mouth and popped a moment before his life force faded away to nothing.

Danny ripped the blade free and turned to face the slowly recovering mercenaries. "You lot can either surrender or die like your employer. What's it going to be?"

The men all tossed their weapons down and raised their hands. It looked like Danny had won this round. Now he had to figure out what he was going to do with all these prisoners.

CHAPTER 18

D anny pushed the final mercenary into the overstuffed cage and locked the door. The wolf pups growled at them but it was more cute than frightening. Keeping them here wasn't a long-term option, but it would suffice until Danny finished searching the outpost. The few details he'd gotten out of the wizard made it clear he needed to visit the city of Discourt next. Finding Avius, assuming that was his real name, would be no easy task. But if he was the mastermind behind the plague, nothing would end until he was eliminated.

"How long are you going to leave us here?" one of the mercenaries asked.

"As long as necessary," Danny said. "If you cause me any trouble, you can stay there forever."

Danny turned, strode out of the lab and turned down a steel hallway. According to the mercenaries, the beastfolk were kept in the basement when they weren't working the field. Getting them sorted out was Danny's priority. Hopefully, all he'd have to do was dispel the marks on their necks. If that didn't work, he'd have to do a bit more research.

The stairs to the basement weren't that far from the lab. Danny pressed one of the glowing runes and the door dropped into the floor. He clanked down the steel steps that went on for far too long for a single story. At last he reached a dirt floor.

His jaw dropped. An immense cavern spread out before him. It was easily ten times the size of the outpost. It looked like it ran all the way to the fields where the beastfolk had been working. A bright-blue crystal embedded in the stone ceiling pulsed in the ether. It had to be the source of the magic that kept the fields warm and fertile. Danny had no idea how to shut it off or even if he should. The magic wasn't doing any harm, at least not as far as he could tell.

Dragging his gaze away from the potent source of magic, Danny focused on the beastfolk slaves that stood around about twenty yards to his right. They gnawed on chunks of raw meat, their blank faces seemingly focused on nothing. The gathering gave off a distinct zombie horror film vibe. Only in this case the zombies were still alive. That made it so much worse.

Danny inched closer, but the beastfolk completely ignored him. It was like they couldn't see him. He shuddered and hoped they weren't aware of their circumstances. That would be a small mercy. At least their lack of reaction made studying the marks on their necks easier.

A faint line of ether ran from the mark up through the ceiling. They weren't attached to the crystal. What, exactly, they were attached to was a question he couldn't answer from here.

Sometimes the easiest path was best. Danny gathered

ether and shaped it into a razor which he used to slice the mark off the nearest beastman's neck. It vanished but only for a moment. Okay, maybe severing the thread would do it.

Danny transformed his razor into a dagger and sliced it through the thread. It passed right through but didn't sever it. All the while he was working, his subject chewed away on a dripping hunk of meat, totally oblivious to the goings-on.

Danny grimaced. He needed to find the source of the thread and deal with it from that end. "I'll be back. Don't worry, I'll find some way to set you free."

Whether his words meant anything to the beastfolk, Danny had no idea. But he didn't want them to feel like he was abandoning them.

Danny retraced his steps, climbing back up to the ground-floor corridor. Now that he knew what to look for, following the threads of ether was fairly simple. Unfortunately, they went right through the floors and walls, causing Danny to frequently lose sight of them. At minimum it was clear they were going to the second floor. The easiest thing would be to go directly there and pick them up again.

Returning to the second-floor stairs, he took them two at a time until he stood once more in the spell circle chamber. Ignoring the wizard's body—he'd already searched it before locking up the mercenaries—he focused with all his will on the ether. The circle put out so much energy it was nearly impossible to see anything else. Working his way slowly around the room, Danny searched for any sign of the threads.

He found them ten minutes later. Their source was a stone cylinder that looked a bit like one of those stamps nobles used to seal a letter with wax, only twice as long. After a moment of hesitation Danny picked it up and flipped it over. Sure enough, on the bottom someone had carved a mark that matched the one on the beastfolk.

It looked like the stamp drew ether in through the bottom before pushing it back out through the mark. Basically it worked like the ethersword. Hardly a surprise since the elves made them both. Assuming he was right, he should be able to shut it off the same way.

Forming a plug of dense ether, Danny covered the bottom of the stamp. A moment later the threads vanished. When he let the plug dissolve, the stamp remained inert. Yup, it worked exactly the same as the ethersword.

Hopefully that meant the beastfolk were free. He put the dangerous artifact into storage and hurried back the way he'd come.

At the bottom of the basement steps he found the beastfolk lurching around like drunks at last call. He kept his distance as they slowly regained their awareness. One of the beastmen, Danny was pretty sure it was the one he'd tried to free, focused his dark-eyed gaze on him.

"You saved us. Why?" the beastman asked.

"Why wouldn't I save you? The mercenaries and their master have caused no end of suffering out in the wider world. I also told Rafe I'd do my best to help the packs that had gone missing. I assume that's you guys."

"I haven't seen Rafe since the last mate swap. Is his pack well?"

"They were when I left them. A group of mercenaries attacked their camp and tried to capture some of the women and young. I happened to be visiting at the time and was able to stop them. That was when Rafe told me about the packs that didn't show up to the last meeting."

The rest of the beastfolk had crowded around Danny as

he was speaking. Their musky, sweaty stink wasn't the most pleasant thing, but he did his best not to let his discomfort show.

"Is this everyone that was taken?" Danny asked.

"No." It seemed the big beastman was going to serve as the group's spokesman. "We were separated from our packs and brought here to work. I have no idea where they took the rest of us."

That wasn't what Danny had been hoping to hear. "I'm sorry. For what it's worth I'll keep looking for your pack mates. I'm Ronin, by the way, an adventurer."

"Val, pack leader of a pack that no longer exists." Val gave a sad shake of his shaggy head. "What happens now?"

"That's up to you. You're all free to do as you wish. My recommendation is that you stay here for the winter. The outpost is secure and warm. You can use the weapons I took from the mercenaries to hunt. I'll show you how to work the doors so you can come and go as you please."

Val let out a little growl. "The mercenaries, you killed them?"

"No, I locked them up. Feel free to do with them as you please. I figure, as the ones most injured by their actions, it's only right that you decide their fate."

Val's smile had more than a little wolf in it. "We will see that they are properly punished. Will you give us some time to make up our minds?"

"By all means. Take as long as you need. There are still a few rooms I need to check. I don't want to leave any dangerous magic behind."

Danny left the beastfolk to their meeting and went back up to the ground floor. There was one hallway he hadn't checked yet, and he was eager to find out what was there. As with all the passages, it was nothing but steel walls with an occasional glowing rune that marked a door.

He opened the first one he reached and found haunches of what he assumed were antelope hanging from hooks. This had to be the source of the beastfolk's rations. He counted at least ten antelopes' worth of meat hanging and ready to eat. That should hold them for a while.

The next room was much more interesting. It was another lab, this one set up for alchemy. Glass vats filled with bubbling blue liquid sat on metal tables. Glowing stones underneath them provided the heat that kept them going.

Off to the side was a neat pile of familiar crates. They looked exactly like the ones in the back of Osbern's wagon. The crates were filled with empty potion bottles, which meant the blue liquid was certainly the plague cure. There was enough here to help a lot of people.

Danny collected everything and put it in his storage. Hopefully Father Sander would have some idea about the best way to distribute it. Some random adventurer handing out cure potions was likely to be met with suspicion. Certainly more suspicion than the temple of the Goddess would be.

That finished his sweep so Danny returned to the basement. Val immediately separated himself from the group and approached. "We have decided to take your suggestion and stay here until the thaw. Some of us are weak from the work. Taking time to recover will be good. When the warm weather comes, if we haven't heard from you, we will begin the search for our missing packmates."

Danny nodded, more than a little relieved they'd made the wise choice. "I found some supplies, let me show you around and how things work. Once you're confident you can manage on your own, I need to return to Redfield."

Val clapped him on the shoulder. "Whatever happens, we will never forget what you did for us. Beastfolk and humans have at times had a strained relationship. What happened here will not help, but you will always be welcome in our territory."

"Thanks. And please, if you can, try not to hold the acts of a few evil men against the rest of us. Most humans want to live a peaceful life, just as your people do."

"For one so young, you speak with the wisdom of a shaman. We shall see what the future holds."

That was fair enough. Danny led the beastfolk upstairs and showed them everything, including the decidedly nervous, locked-up mercenaries. When the tour was over, he and Val parted ways with a final handshake. Each of them had one of the stone cylinders that activated the outpost door. That would make it easier for Danny when he hopefully brought back the missing beastfolk.

For now it was time to return to Redfield and plan his next move.

CHAPTER 19

Danny never expected to feel relief at the sight of Redfield, but he kind of did. He'd spent enough time in the town that he felt a certain connection to the place. It wasn't home, but it was close.

The western gate was open and a small detachment of guards along with a dark-robed priest of the Binder were on duty. Looked like the security situation had returned to pre-outbreak levels. That was a good sign. The lack of travelers was likely due to the time of year. If it was above freezing today, he'd eat his sword.

When he was ten yards out, the guards formed up, presenting a wall of spears. "Identify yourself and state your business in Redfield," the lead guard said.

"Ronin, elite adventurer. I've got an Alpha Wolf pelt to turn in at the guild." He stuck to the truth just in case the priest was using a lie detection spell.

The priest nodded. "He's free of disease."

That announcement made the guards slump with relief. It might have been comical if the situation were different.

"Go on in," the guard said. "And welcome to Redfield."

"Much obliged, gentlemen."

Danny strode through the gate and headed straight for the Golden Gate Inn. He wanted to check on Lise, take a bath, and enjoy a hot meal before he went to see Father Sander. Danny couldn't smell himself anymore, but between the walking and fighting, he doubted he was at his best.

It was good to see the market open and busy. Vendors called out for customers and heavily bundled shoppers haggled for items. Danny nodded in passing to a woman waving and offering wool scarves. They looked nice and warm but he wasn't in the market for a new scarf.

Before long he reached the tavern. It was midmorning so that should mean he'd arrived between the breakfast and lunch crowd. Pushing through the door he found the common room every bit as empty as he'd hoped.

By the bar, Lise laughed at something Emile said. She leaned in close to him and he touched her hand. Danny grinned. Love, it seemed, had blossomed during his absence. Good, if she'd gotten over whatever crush she had on him that suited Danny well.

He closed the door a little harder than strictly necessary and both of the lovebirds started and looked his way. "Hey. You both look fully recovered."

Lise blushed and Emile winced.

"We were just...um..." Emile trailed off, clearly unsure about the situation.

"Relax." Danny took a seat at the bar. "Lise and I are just friends. She looked as happy as I've seen her since we met when I came in. That fact makes me very happy."

"Ronin." Lise hugged him. "I wasn't sure how you'd react.

Emile has been wonderful these past few days. I feel like I'm alive again."

Danny patted her hand. "I'm glad to hear it. Any chance I can get a hot bath and something to eat? It's been a rough few days."

"Absolutely!" Emile said. "I'll fetch the tub and have the girls put some water on to heat. No charge of course."

The bartender hurried away and Danny could only shake his head at the change in the man. "What does he think I am, your father?"

"I told him it would be fine." Lise sat on the stool beside Danny. "But since we came in together and you were so protective of me, he believed there was something there despite my assurances."

"Given his attitude when we arrived, I'm surprised you two hit it off."

"We caught him at a bad time. Emile is very sweet. He's been kind to me, in a different way than you have."

Danny knew exactly what she meant. "I'm glad it worked out for you. I take it you'll be staying in Redfield."

"I was leaning that way before there was anything between Emile and me. This just solidified my decision. Thank you for getting me this far. I'll be grateful for all you did until my last breath."

"It was my pleasure."

Emile emerged from the kitchen lugging the heavy tub. Danny took pity on the man and grabbed an end. Together they lugged it upstairs and into his room.

When it was set up Emile said, "The water won't be long."

"Thanks. Emile." When the bartender finally looked Danny in the eye he said, "I only want her to be happy. If you can give her that, I'll wish you the best. If you break her heart, I'll make you wish the plague had killed you."

The blood drained from Emile's face. "I'd never do anything to hurt her, I swear. I've never loved anyone the way I do Lise."

Danny smiled. "Glad to hear it. Finding true love is a rare and wonderful gift."

The serving girls arrived a moment later and Danny settled in to take a nice, long soak.

After his bath and a hot meal, Danny left the inn and headed across town to the temple of the Goddess. The lack of a line of sick people brought a smile to Danny's face. As he'd hoped, the potions appeared to have turned the tide.

He slipped inside and checked the chapel. No sign of Father Sander. If the high priest wasn't here, he had to be in the infirmary. That he might be resting never occurred to Danny. The good father struck him as the sort who worked himself to the edge of exhaustion.

Sure enough, he found Father Sander tending a shivering woman whose gaunt face shone with fever sweat. At least she was the only patient at the moment. Thank heaven for small favors. When the priest looked his way Danny gave a little wave. He waved back and shuffled over. The poor guy didn't look like he'd slept in a week.

"Ronin, welcome back. How did your mission go?"

Danny filled him in on the details. "I've got about ten gallons of cure potion. Doesn't look like you need it here. I figure my best bet is to have the Discourt temple handle distribution."

"A wise decision. Going through the temple will be much easier and more efficient. I can't leave Redfield, but I'll send

Michael with you, along with a letter of explanation. The high priestess in Discourt, Mother Ankie, is a good person. You can trust her to do the right thing."

"Much obliged, Father."

"We should be thanking you, not the other way around. I can't imagine what we would've done had you not arrived and stepped in to help."

"What did you end up doing with Osbern and his thugs?"

"They're still in jail. Once things are fully back to normal, we'll hold a trial. Since they'll be forced to answer under the effects of a truth spell, I fear the results will not be in their favor. The requirements of justice will likely see them swinging from a noose by the end of the week." Father Sander sounded a bit sad about it. As far as Danny was concerned it was a well-deserved punishment.

"Will you have Michael meet me at the west gate at first light?" Danny asked.

"Of course. You can use Osbern's wagon and team for the trip. The temple has confiscated it as part of his punishment."

Danny could make better time on foot, but traveling with Michael it would probably be prudent to have transportation. "That works for me. Try to get some rest, Father. You look all in."

Father Sander chuckled. "I've been getting plenty of sleep. It's the constant magic use that's wearing me out."

"I can help with that." Danny opened his storage and pulled out a potion. "Give her this and send her home to rest."

Father Sander took the potion and offered a weary smile. "I believe I will. Goddess bless you, Ronin."

"Take it easy, Father." They shook hands and left the

temple. He wanted to swing by the Adventurers' Guild and see how Reggie and the secretaries were doing.

It didn't take long to walk to the guild and when he arrived he could hear voices inside. Sounded like some of the adventurers had returned from their missions. That was good. It would make things livelier. A quiet guild was just depressing.

He pushed through the door and glanced around at the handful of occupied tables. Men and women in armor were drinking and laughing. If you didn't know a plague was going around, you'd be forgiven for thinking all was normal.

Danny nodded to the few who looked his way as he walked to the counter. The woman on duty offered a bright smile when he arrived.

"Welcome back, Ronin. The guild master said you healed us. Thank you so much. I really thought I was going to die for a while."

"I'm glad I could help. I've got an Alpha Wolf hide and skull I'd like to turn in if that's okay."

"Absolutely, let's see it."

Danny opened his storage and placed the pelt and skull on the counter.

"That's from an Alpha Wolf?" Her astonished question drew the attention of every adventurer in the room and soon Danny was surrounded by curious onlookers who were gaping at the huge skull.

"Yes. According to the beastfolk hunters I spoke to there's a new, larger, more aggressive breed moving into the area. It's about the size of a full-grown horse and way quicker than anything so big should be. If you're hunting them, you'll want to be extra careful. Hell, even if you're only on a guard job, you'll want to keep an eye out for these things."

The crowd broke up into muttering groups and Danny focused on the secretary. "Is it going to be a problem?"

"No, no problem, but I can't give you any extra for the skull. I can bump up the price for the pelt by twenty-five percent since it's so big."

"That's fine," Danny said. "I don't suppose bringing it in counts as a successful mission for promotion purposes?"

"Sorry, these sorts of standing bounty offers aren't really missions. We post them as a way for our members to make money when they're having trouble finding a job that's a good fit for their skills."

"Makes sense," Danny said. "If Reggie's free I'd like to have a word with him."

"I'll check. As far as I know he's not busy right now. Just a moment." The secretary quick walked through the hall back to the guild master's office.

Danny had left a fair bit out of the story for the masses but figured the boss man needed to know everything. Well, most everything.

After a brief wait the secretary returned with a small pouch in hand. "You can go on back. Here's your payment for the wolf."

"Thanks." He put the pouch in his satchel and strode back to Reggie's office. He knocked twice and said, "It's Ronin."

"Come in." Reggie was seated behind his desk looking far healthier than the last time Danny saw him. "What's on your mind?"

"I've got some news I'm not sure should be made public. Father Sander knows already. I figure I'll pass it along and you can decide between the two of you what you want to share."

"Sounds serious." Reggie steepled his fingers. "Go ahead, please."

Danny laid it all out and when he finished added, "Anything you can tell me about Discourt in general and Avius in particular would be most helpful."

"The name Avius means nothing to me," Reggie said. "I spend as little time in the city as I can. It's a cesspool. The city lords are constantly competing for power and influence. The guilds are little better, even ours. The temples do their best, but even they are far from pure. The best advice I can offer is to watch your back. Oh, and talk to Berend, he's the assistant guild master and a straight arrow. Frankly, he's the only person in the whole stinking city I trust."

"I wasn't sure what to expect, but from what you've described, the situation is worse than I feared. Dealing with a crazy wizard and a plague is bad enough, but throw feuding lords into the mix and it gets even crazier."

"You know this isn't your responsibility, right?" Reggie asked. "You've already done more than anyone could expect from a random adventurer."

"You might be right, but if I don't do it, who will?" Danny shook his head. "I took the job from Mayor Rik and, unofficial or not, I plan to see it through. Could you write me a letter of introduction to Berend? It'll give me an excuse to talk to him when I arrive."

"Sure, not a problem." Reggie dug around in his desk, a disgruntled look wrinkling up his face. "You know, it's kind of pathetic that the guild master can't even do close to as much as a newbie adventurer."

Danny grinned. "I'm sure you did your share when you were an adventurer. It's my turn now. Try not to let it bother you."

Whether Danny's little speech made Reggie feel better he had no idea. He hoped it did. The guild master seemed like a decent fellow and the world needed more of them.

Letter in hand, Danny left for the inn. He was getting an early start tomorrow and he wanted to get as much rest as possible. From what he'd heard about Discourt, he'd need to be at his best if he didn't want the city to eat him alive.

CHAPTER 20

Discourt was the first proper city Danny had seen since leaving the Five Kingdoms. From a distance, he guessed it was about the same size as Forte City. Huge stone walls with towers at regular intervals protected it. Nothing less than a serious army would threaten those walls. And even then he couldn't imagine how many lives a traditional siege would cost.

The city sat right on the Western Trade Road, just like Redfield. There was also a gate to the north where a small road ran. Hundreds of farms, their fallow fields covered with a light layer of snow, surrounded the city.

At the main gate, a modest line waited to enter. There were three wagons loaded with firewood along with two parties on foot. Not a ton of activity, but for this time of year it was better than nothing.

"I can't wait to get off this bench and go somewhere warm," Michael said. "A mug of mulled wine wouldn't go amiss either."

Danny couldn't argue with the sentiment. Two weeks of

traveling on the hard wagon bench from dawn until dusk was rough on the backside. They'd avoided all the little towns they passed on the way. The people would no doubt have many questions and neither of them was eager to provide answers. It also would've slowed them down and Danny was eager to reach the city and continue his search for the mysterious Avius.

"If you can find a good place," Danny said. "The first round is on me."

Michael sighed. "Unfortunately I think we'd best go straight to the temple and report to the high priestess."

"Good call."

Michael flicked the reins and the wagon clattered down to join the line to enter Discourt. As with the smaller towns, there was a squad of guards along with a priest checking everyone before giving them permission to enter. It was a standard and now familiar ritual. None of the people ahead of them were refused and then it was Danny and Michael's turn.

The guard spokesman raised a gauntleted hand and said, "State your names and business."

"I'm Michael, a priest of the Goddess on my way to the temple. The man beside me is Ronin, an adventurer guarding me on my journey."

Danny offered a polite nod but stayed quiet. They'd decided to let Michael take the lead since his position as a priest should afford him greater deference.

The guard looked back at the priest on duty, a heavily bundled up woman whose face was the only thing visible, who said, "They're free from disease."

"There's no entry fee for priests," the guard said. "But your guard will have to pay five silvers."

That was sufficiently cheap that Danny paid without comment.

"Much obliged and welcome to Discourt." The guard waved them through and Michael urged the horses into motion.

Immediately past the gate, peddlers by the dozens hawked their wares. Anything you could think of was for sale. The scent of cooking meat caught Danny's attention. He spotted a food vendor selling sausages on a stick.

Danny whistled and when the vendor looked his way he held up two fingers. The man gave a thumbs-up and hurried over with two sausages. "Two silvers, sir."

Danny handed him the coins and took the food. The transfer happened without stopping the wagon. Judging by the way he handled it, the vendor had a lot of experience. Michael took one of the sausages and they dug in.

The first bite burned Danny's mouth, both from the temperature and the spices. The sausage was the most flavorsome thing he'd eaten since arriving on this world and it was delicious. He glanced at Michael and nearly burst out laughing. Tears were running down the man's cheeks. Perhaps it was too spicy for him.

"Is it good?" Danny asked.

"A bit on the spicy side, but not bad. We don't get sausages like this in Redfield."

Danny grinned but made no further comment. The wagon trundled down the city's main street. Eventually they left the crowded market behind and entered a more traditional business area with shops and taverns. There were a few people out and about, but they were hurrying to their destinations, puffs of white filling the air with each breath.

"How long does it stay cold around here?" Danny asked.

"Four to six weeks for the really bad stuff. It'll be chilly for another month after that followed by a few weeks of mud and black flies. Then spring planting."

That wasn't bad, especially compared to Sentinel City back home. They usually got at least four months of cold weather and several feet of snow. You got used to it eventually but that didn't make it pleasant.

"Do you know where you're going?" Danny asked.

"Sure. Father Sander gave me directions before we left. When we reach the central district we turn right and follow Temple Street right to it. The Goddess's temple is the biggest in the city so it shouldn't be hard to spot."

"Does the temple serve as an infirmary here as well?"

"Yup. That's our calling, after all. Everyone is welcome at the temple."

"If you heal for free, how do you make a living?"

"Easy, we charge for house calls. The people with money don't want to go out when they're sick, so they'll send a servant with an offering and we'll send a healer back with them. The bigger the offering, the higher the rank of priest we send. There are fewer people willing to pay for a house call in Redfield, but plenty of people will make a small offering when they're healed, so we manage. Here's the turn."

The buildings had been getting nicer by the minute. The central district was filled with mansions. Happily, they'd be turning off before entering that lofty area. They reached an intersection labeled with several signs, one of which said Temple Street which Michael turned down.

They hadn't gone far when Danny spotted jutting gray spires flanking a bell tower. Below the tower was a door marked with the inverted sword of Branik. The rest of the temple was utilitarian gray stone with minimal decorations.

It had a very fortress-like look which was perfect for the Sword Lord.

A little ways past Branik's temple they came to a massive, sprawling stone building that had to be the Goddess's temple. Since they also served as hospitals, they were always the largest temple in any town. At least there was no line of sick people outside, which Danny took as a good sign.

So far it appeared the plague hadn't gotten its hooks into Discourt. Maybe Avius didn't want the results of his experiment showing up in his backyard. Or maybe it was dumb luck. Danny meant to find out one way or the other.

Michael pulled the wagon off to the side of the street in front of the temple and threw the brake. No steps led up to the doors, no doubt to make it easier for sick people to enter.

They climbed down from the bench and Danny asked, "Will the wagon be okay out here?"

"In the temple district? It should be fine. Come on." Michael led the way to the front door and pushed through.

There was a small entry room with a young woman dressed in the familiar white robes of the order seated behind a modest desk with a book and pen on top. She smiled at them and asked, "Are you here to pray or do you require healing?"

"Neither," Michael said. "I'm from the Redfield temple and my companion and I need to speak to Mother Ankie on a matter of some urgency."

"What sort of matter?" the priestess asked.

"A plague-related one," Michael said.

She chewed her lip and looked over her shoulder at the blank wall. What she was hoping to see there was beyond Danny. The room had two exits, one to the left and one to the right. Straight ahead was solid stone.

"Is there a problem with us speaking to her?" Michael asked.

"Ah, well..." The priestess trailed off, looking far more uncomfortable than such a simple question warranted.

"If there's a problem," Danny said, speaking for the first time. "Perhaps we can help. I'm an adventurer and have some skill with magic."

She looked all around again before lowering her voice. "Mother Ankie collapsed three days ago after healing a plague victim. We haven't had many and she's the only priest strong enough to cure them. The treatment went well, but only minutes later she collapsed and hasn't woken since. The clergy are beside themselves as no form of magical healing has roused her."

"Let me take a look," Danny said. "If priestly magic isn't sufficient maybe a different approach will have more success."

"I can't let a complete stranger into our most inner sanctum."

"Ronin has done great things for Redfield," Michael said. "I'll vouch for both his ability and honor. If the situation is as dire as you say, the greater risk lies in not accepting the help of someone who could make a difference."

"I'll get the acting high priest, Father Koen. It's up to him to decide who sees Mother Ankie. Excuse me." She got up and hurried out the right-hand door. Danny caught a glimpse of the chapel before the door closed behind her.

"What do you think?" Danny asked. "I was under the impression that followers of the Goddess were immune to disease."

"We are, it's a divine blessing. If Mother Ankie caught something despite that, it's no wonder the priests are upset.

A disease dangerous enough to overcome the protection of an archangel could wipe out the whole city."

"Yeah, and yet it sounds like the high priestess is the only one who's sick. Could a disease be that dangerous and at the same time not contagious?"

Michael let out a weak laugh. "You're asking a low-ranking priest from a small town in the middle of nowhere. I'm hardly an expert. In fact, you probably know more about it than I do."

"I don't know much about diseases, but I do know that it sounds like she was poisoned rather than sickened. You're not immune to poison, right?"

The blood had drained from Michael's face. "No, we're not. But who would want to poison the only priest capable of curing the... plague."

"See it now? The people spreading it might like that very much."

"Heaven's mercy."

"Yup. Hopefully someone got a good look at the last person she healed. A name and an address would be nice as well since I'd very much like to have a chat with him or her."

The young lady returned with an older man in white robes marked with a red cross. He looked about sixty and had dark ridges under his eyes and a sallow complexion. Clearly the man hadn't been sleeping well.

"I'm Father Koen," the older man said. "Sister Katie says you want to try and help our high priestess. What makes you think your magic will succeed where the Goddess's blessing has failed?"

He didn't sound angry, just totally exhausted and at his wit's end. Perfectly understandable given the circumstances.

"My magic works differently than priestly healing,"

Danny said. "Maybe it'll work and maybe it won't. The only way to say for sure is to try. I'm willing to do so for free. What do you have to lose?"

"You make a compelling argument, Ronin, was it? Mother Ankie is getting weaker by the day and all our magic can do is prolong her life, not cure her. Soon we won't even be able to manage that much. If you can do anything to help, I would be remiss in my duties not to let you try. Follow me." Father Koen turned back to the chapel door.

When Michael tried to follow them, Father Koen said, "Only Ronin for now. We're limiting access in case anyone else might be susceptible to whatever she has. Your patience is appreciated."

Michael bowed. "Of course, Father. May I pray in the chapel?"

"By all means. Any prayers are welcome."

Danny and Father Koen passed between the pews and past the altar through a door that led deeper into the temple. When they were alone Danny said, "I was speaking to Michael earlier. I have a theory about Mother Ankie's illness."

"Oh?"

"I don't think she's sick. I think the last person she healed poisoned her."

"Impossible! Mother Ankie is the most beloved figure in the city. No one would want to kill her."

"The people spreading the plague might," Danny said.

Father Koen stopped and turned to face him. "I'm not sure I understand."

Danny gave him an abbreviated update on what he'd learned so far. "The plague isn't spreading naturally.

Someone wants this to happen. Someone named Avius. Does the name mean anything to you?"

Father Koen shook his head, seeming unable to speak. At last he asked, "Why, in heaven's name, would anyone want to do something so evil?"

"I don't know, Father, but when I find him, I'll be sure to ask. Anyway, it occurred to me that removing the only priest in the city capable of curing the disease might be high on Avius's to-do list."

"Indeed." Father Koen resumed walking. "This news certainly casts the current situation in a darker light. Still, even if it was poison, our magic should've been able to purge it. The idea of a poison resistant to divine healing is terrifying."

"Everything about our situation is terrifying," Danny said. "While I'm glad I've been able to unravel some of it, there's still much left to do."

They reached a door with a pair of knights in mail armor standing in front of it. One of them hastened to open the door when he and Father Koen were close. "No one has entered since your last visit, Father."

"That is well, thank you. We will be attempting a new healing. Make sure we're not disturbed."

Both knights shot Danny professional glares but there was no real heat in them. He was here in the company of the acting leader of the temple. If that failed to make it clear he had permission, nothing would.

They slipped inside and the guard closed the door silently behind them. There wasn't much of interest in the room aside from the bed and its unconscious occupant. Mother Ankie looked about sixty to Danny, though that might have been a side effect of her illness as her complexion was pale, her cheeks hollow, and her hair white. On the nightstand beside her rested a pitcher and bowl. And that was it. There wasn't even a chair for a visitor.

"Can I do anything to help?" Father Koen asked.

"I can't think of anything. I'm going to take a valuable artifact out of my personal storage. If you could avoid mentioning it to anyone, that would be great." Danny pulled the ethersword out of storage.

"What is it?" Father Koen asked. "It looks like a silver sword hilt. Is it dedicated to Branik?"

"It's not silver, it's mithril, an artifact of the ancient elf-bloods. It can enhance my magic to a limited degree. Please be quiet while I'm concentrating."

"Of course, forgive me."

Danny cast a ward around himself then put the priest out of his mind. Some people would no doubt claim he was paranoid, but Danny didn't know Father Koen, not really, and to give this his best effort would require his full concentration. Which in turn would leave him vulnerable should anyone want to stab him in the back of the head.

He took a deep breath and drew ether through the mithril, infused it with holy energy, then sent it back out into Mother Ankie. Just as he did when he cured the plague victims, Danny charged every cell in her body with ether while destroying everything that didn't belong. It wasn't a conscious effort. He pictured the result he wanted then trusted the magic to make his desire reality.

The room flooded with white light and a moment later Danny found himself floating amidst white clouds. In the distance, a golden gate guarded by huge lions that looked like they could eat an Alpha Wolf for breakfast made it clear where he was. As if the gates of Heaven weren't enough of a clue, a moment after his arrival, a beautiful woman with the wings of a dove and holding a golden staff appeared before him.

"Goddess?" he guessed. Hopefully it wasn't Adonael. He had no desire to deal with the archangel again.

"Correct, Daniel." Her voice was as beautiful as the rest of her. "Thank you for saving my high priestess. She is a remarkable human, kinder than any three of you combined."

"You're welcome. I'm glad the magic worked. I'm assuming you didn't bring me here just to say thanks. If you're planning to pick up where Adonael left off, you can save yourself some time. I'm not hunting down the demon king and I'm not giving up on destroying the summoning circle."

"I have no intention of asking you to. The game was the only way to save Valindor from Null's wrath, but I never approved of dragging innocents into the fight. It should've been a matter for a local champion to handle. Adonael saw a way to increase our side's chances of winning and deemed the loss of a handful of mortals acceptable for the greater good. It saddens me that many of my fellows agreed with her."

"Okay, so what did you want?" Danny asked.

"Only to warn you. There are vast dangers in the world. For all your considerable power, you are far from the strongest being on Valindor."

Danny frowned. "I was told the demon king and I were the two strongest beings in the world."

"You were misled," she said. "You were told that to drive home the threat of the demon king and to give you confidence you could beat her."

So it was all a lie. The truth surprised him less than he would've liked. "Is Avius one of these greater threats?"

"I can't speak directly about a mortal matter. If I help you, other powers will then be free to help Avius. Better to let you handle it on your own."

"I appreciate your consideration, Goddess. It's more than I expected from anyone in Heaven."

She let out a long sigh. "It saddens me to hear you say that, but I also understand. Take care of yourself, Daniel. If you are to succeed, you will have to walk a long, dark path. Don't let it take your humanity. Don't let it darken your heart."

Danny blinked and found himself looking down into the electric-blue eyes of Mother Ankie. "Who are you?"

Before Danny could answer, Father Koen rushed over and fell to his knees beside the bed. "We've been so worried, Ankie. You've been unconscious for three days."

"Three days?" She sounded almost comically confused. "The last thing I remember was healing that unfortunate woman. I felt dizzy for a moment, then nothing."

"I'm pretty sure she poisoned you," Danny said. "Do you know who she was?"

"Ronin! You can't interrogate the high priestess immediately after her recovery. She needs time to regain her strength."

"It's alright," she said. "No, I don't know her name. She was a young woman, perhaps twenty-five at most. Rather pretty, with long blond hair, pale skin, and green eyes. I'm afraid that's all I can remember."

"That's helpful," Danny said, more to be polite than because it actually was. "I noticed a book in the entrance. Would she have signed it?"

"Possibly," Father Koen said. "But if she was in an especially poor condition, signing in might have been skipped. It happens. No more for now. Ankie needs to rest."

"Something to eat would be better than rest," she said.

"Of course," Father Koen said. "I'll have soup and bread brought at once. It's so good to have you back."

"It's good to be back. And I want it known that Ronin is welcome to come visit me anytime he wishes."

Father Koen made a face. "Are you sure that's a good idea?"

"I am. He has the Goddess's blessing. Can you not feel it? She has touched him."

"Him?" Danny felt every bit as incredulous as Father Koen sounded.

"Indeed. With Ronin here, I have every confidence this vile disease will finally be eradicated for good."

Danny would certainly do his best, but he hoped her faith wasn't misplaced. "I need to swing by the Adventurers' Guild anyway. I'll stop by in the morning and we can have a proper chat."

"I'd like that." Mother Ankie's smile was radiant. "And thank you for saving my life."

"It was my pleasure. Until tomorrow." Danny offered a short bow and turned for the door, Father Koen at his heels.

"Are you truly blessed by the Goddess?" Father Koen asked when they were alone.

"I don't know about blessed, but I spoke to her during the healing. All the holy energy I channeled must have opened a path to Heaven. She wasn't especially helpful."

"No. Heaven prefers to let us handle our problems on our own. What I wouldn't give to speak with her. I will spread the word. Rest assured you will be made welcome anytime you wish to return."

"Thanks."

They found Michael deep in conversation with the cute priestess on duty. He had good taste in women, Danny had to give him that.

"Mother Ankie?" the priestess asked.

"Healed and hungry," Father Koen said. "I'm going to find her something to eat. By her order, Ronin is to be allowed to visit anytime."

"As you say, Father." She bowed.

As Father Koen started to leave Danny said, "Best make sure to check all of her food for poison."

"No one in the temple would ever harm Ankie," Father Koen said.

"It's your call, but I wouldn't risk it. See you tomorrow." Turning to Michael, Danny asked, "Are you coming with me or staying here?"

"I'll stay here unless you need me for something."

Danny grinned. "No, you two have fun. Don't forget to move the wagon. Oh, before I forget, did the woman Mother Ankie healed sign the ledger?"

The priestess shook her head. "I was on duty when she came in. Two men carried her on a stretcher. There was no way she had the strength to sign."

That was convenient, for her. "Thanks. See you later."

He left the two lovebirds alone and set out for the guild. A beautiful blond assassin should be easy to find, but somehow he doubted it would be so simple.

CHAPTER 21

Danny left the temple of the Goddess and stepped out into the cold, bright afternoon. He blinked a couple times to let his eyes adjust to the glare. What the Goddess had said about him and the demon king not being as strong as everyone claimed, while far from a huge surprise, did plant a kernel of doubt in Danny's mind.

Was he going to be able to complete the task he'd set for himself? He didn't know. Like any other mission, he would do the best he could. That was all anyone could do. Hopefully it would be enough. If it wasn't, at least Lyra was there to help the next guy. Hopefully she wouldn't feel the need to murder him after he won.

"Ah, shit!" Danny completely forgot to ask where to find the Adventurers' Guild. Discourt was way bigger than Redfield. He doubted he'd have much luck finding the place on his own.

He walked back the way he'd come. If he remembered right there had been guards on duty at Branik's temple.

Followers of the Sword Lord should know where to find the Adventurers' Guild.

A short walk brought him to the intimidating stone fortress that served as Branik's temple. The place definitely screamed, "we worship an archangel devoted to battle." Two armed guards stood shivering on either side of the arched entrance. Danny wasn't sure if it was some kind of punishment or training, but standing around in this weather had to suck.

He moved closer, careful to keep his hands well away from his sword. "Excuse me, fellas. I need to find the Adventurers' Guild. Could you tell me where it is?"

The guards looked at each other, seeming uncertain if they should speak to him. Maybe they were like the royal guards in the Kingdom of the Isles back home. They weren't supposed to speak to the tourists who stopped to take pictures with them.

Of course, Danny had spoken to a couple of the royal guards when they were off duty during a deployment to the Kingdom and both men admitted that if a cute girl wanted a picture they would try and get her number.

After their moment of contemplation one of the guards said, "You're pretty far off. The guild is all the way on the other side of the city. Follow the main road west until you reach the big statue of Adonael. Take a right on Blade Street and keep going until you see the guild. They've got a big sign out front. You can't miss it."

"Thanks," Danny said. "Try and stay warm."

"You got a sick sense of humor," the other guard said. "Anyone ever tell you that?"

"It's possible I've heard something along those lines before. So long, fellas."

Danny set out, boots crunching on the snow. He didn't mind the walk. It would keep him warm and might give him a chance to overhear some useful gossip. Someone had to be talking about the plague. Though if they knew anything genuinely useful it would be a pleasant surprise.

He left the temple district, keeping to the main road running due west. It was basically the Western Trade Road. The city sat right on it. Seemed a bit arrogant to Danny, building your city right on a major trade route, but they weren't the only ones to do it. You'd think they could've built it off to one side at least. Of course, if they'd done that, the people in charge might have lost out on some taxes, and no one wanted that.

The streets were quiet, no doubt thanks to the cold. The few people Danny saw hurried along, head down, their breath steaming in the air. Maybe his idea about eavesdropping wasn't such a good one after all.

He spotted a general store and ducked inside. A cast iron stove in the middle of the showroom put out a lovely heat. A dozen people were perusing the shelves. Everything you could ever want was on display, from fifty-pound bags of corn to swords to brooms.

Danny eased his way around the room, pausing near a group of three middle-aged women near a stack of shirts.

"I heard Mother Ankie took ill and was in a coma," one of the women said. "Don't know if it's the plague or not."

"Can't be the plague," another woman said. "She has the Goddess's blessing. There's no way she'd ever end up sick. Poor thing probably overworked herself."

The discussion moved on to the price of wool so Danny continued browsing. Not that he wanted anything other than to eavesdrop. And after a couple more stops he didn't even want to do that anymore. The sorts of tedious, mundane stuff people discussed never ceased to amaze him.

He kept moving steadily west, stopping here and there to listen, seldom hearing anything interesting. Mother Ankie's health problems were the primary relevant subject of discussion. No doubt everyone would be quite relieved when word got out that she'd recovered.

When he reached the statue of Adonael—Danny would've sworn the thing's eyes watched him as he strode past—he decided to check one more place before the guild. He settled on a blacksmith shop. Inside there was a little showroom with a mixture of weapons and tools for sale.

Two men dressed in leather armor were standing beside the arrowheads. Danny took them for hunters, though they might've been adventurers. He went to the nearby dagger rack and picked up a straight-bladed dirk that brought back bad memories.

"I'm telling you," the nearest hunter said. "Two guys in black armor were dragging off a coughing kid and I doubt they were taking her to the Goddess's temple."

"Why would anyone want to get close to someone with the plague, much less touch them? You're nuts. It was probably some rich merchant's kid they were bringing home."

"If that was a rich kid she was the worst-dressed rich kid I've ever seen. I'll bet the lord mayor is grabbing up and getting rid of anyone sick. You know he won't want the city locked down."

"I don't want the city locked down," the dubious hunter said. "Venison's bringing good money right now and the price will stay high for a couple more months. Gotta make our coin while the getting is good."

"You've got a point. Still, that black armor gave me the creeps. Let's get out of here."

The hunters took ten arrowheads to the counter and paid for them. Danny returned the dagger to its place and continued his walk. The story about the black-armored men gave him demon king vibes, but the plague didn't seem like the sort of thing Ardent Lilly's cult would be interested in.

Likely as not it was just a misunderstanding. Still, wouldn't hurt to mention the story to Berend. He might be able to confirm the existence of the black-armored soldiers.

The Discourt Adventurers' Guild put every other guild Danny had visited to shame. Not that it was especially fancy, but it was huge. It covered a full city block and had three stories. The sign of the crossed sword and wand was more like a billboard. A blind man could've seen it plain as day.

As he approached, the heavy oak-and-iron doors swung open. A trio of broad-shouldered warriors came sauntering out. They carried war-axes and wore breastplates over heavy woolen winter gear. They barely glanced at him as they ambled past arguing over who was going to drink whom under the table.

Their raucous laughter faded as Danny stepped through the open door. The high-ceilinged waiting room was abuzz with activity. A dozen adventurers were waiting in three lines while other groups sat at tables planning their next job. The place had a totally different vibe than any of the guilds he'd visited before. There was a liveliness that had been missing elsewhere.

The threat of war and plague at the other guilds no doubt played a part in the gloomy atmosphere. Though you'd think that would apply here since the plague was literally on Discourt's doorstep if not already in the foyer.

Well, whatever. He had a job to do and he'd best get at it. Danny approached the counter and got in line. Since they were all the same length, he chose the rightmost line. Mostly because it had the cutest secretary. It also had a speedy line and fifteen minutes later he stepped up to a pretty brunette and offered his best smile.

"Are you here to register?" she asked before Danny could even open his mouth.

"No, ma'am." Danny put his guild badge on the counter. "I was asked to deliver a letter to someone named Berend by Guild Master Reggie at the Redfield Guild."

"If it's from a guild master it must be important," she said.

"It might be," Danny agreed. "I haven't read it. Is Berend available?"

"As far as I know he has no more meetings today. Have a seat and I'll make sure." She motioned to the unoccupied tables.

"Thanks." Danny settled at a small round table while she hurried to a nearby set of stairs and climbed up.

No one approached him and that suited Danny fine. He had zero interest in chitchat at the moment. Now that he was close to delivering his message he wanted to get it done and see if Berend had any information for him.

The wait was blessedly short. The secretary returned and hurried over to his table. "Berend is free and would be pleased to meet with you. This way."

Danny stood and followed her up the stairs to the second floor then down a hall. "He's not on the third floor?"

"Oh, no. The third floor is exclusively for the guild master." She made a face when she mentioned the guild master, kind of like she'd bitten into a lemon. "He meets with rich and powerful clients up there so everything has to be kept just right."

Sounded like the guild master was a snob, but Danny kept his opinion to himself. He had no interest or need to meet with him, especially since everything he'd heard made him suspect the guy was a crook at minimum.

The secretary knocked on a closed door and said, "Ronin to see you, sir."

A whip-thin man without a hair on his face or head opened the door, looked Danny over, and said, "Welcome. Please come in. Thank you, Lauren, that's all for now."

She bowed. "Yes, sir."

Lauren trotted off and Danny entered the office. It looked lived in. Papers covered the desk, a bookcase was stuffed to bursting with books and mementos, and one of the two guest chairs was piled high with outdoor gear.

Berend sat behind his desk and Danny handed him the message before taking the empty chair.

"Anything I should know before I read this?" Berend asked.

"I'm not sure what Reggie wrote. Better if you read it then we can compare notes and ask our questions."

"Fair enough." Berend fell silent and unrolled the scroll. Danny could almost tell what he was reading by the twitches on his face. Berend wouldn't make it as a professional poker player, that was certain.

At last he set the scroll down. "This is... something. Did you really defeat a wizard, free a bunch of beastfolk slaves, and find gallons of cure potion?"

"Yes. I also tracked the potential source of the plague to this city in the form of a man named Avius. Does that mean anything to you?"

Berend shook his head. "It's not a family name, not a prominent one anyway. Where did you hear it?"

"The wizard I killed said his master's name was Avius and that he plucked him out of the Discourt school of magic." Berend snorted a laugh. "Did I say something funny?"

"No, sorry. But saying Discourt has a school of magic is being overly generous. The Wizards' Guild offers classes to anyone who shows magical potential. It's a fine way to earn the goodwill of future members. Calling it a school is a stretch. I'll wager your dead wizard was one of the advanced students. The guild will take on a few promising students as research assistants."

"Seems a trip to the Wizards' Guild needs to go on my itinerary."

"I wouldn't get your hopes up. They're very tight-lipped about their members."

"Even mass murderers?"

"Maybe they'll surprise me, but I doubt it. I can write you a letter of introduction. Our guilds work closely together since many adventurers are members of both. It should secure you a meeting at least."

"I appreciate it," Danny said. "Reggie was right, you are a good guy. I was warned that Discourt wasn't known for its large population of honorable men."

Berend laughed again. "That's one way to put it. Discourt is where honor goes to die. Sometimes literally. Be careful which hornets' nests you poke."

"Thanks for the warning, but I'm not going to figure out where Avius is by keeping quiet. If I have to poke a hundred nests, I will. I've seen too many dead people to let it go."

"That's fair. I won't mention your visit to the guild

master. That should help some." Berend took out a blank strip of paper and started writing.

"Is he one of the less than honorable ones?"

"You could put it that way. Lars would sell his mother for a silver coin. Though, having met his mother, I'm not sure I'd blame him. Anyway, the less you have to do with him, the better. I'll make sure the girls know that you can see me whenever you need to."

"One more question if you don't mind."

"Go ahead."

Danny told him about the black-armored men he heard about. "Is there any truth to the rumor?"

"There might be. Nothing would surprise me after ten years in Discourt. But I don't have any proof they're real." Berend handed him a rolled-up scroll. "There. Keep me informed. If I can help, I will."

"Thanks." They shook hands and Danny took his leave. He wanted to find a good inn and get some rest. Looked like tomorrow was going to be another busy day.

CHAPTER 22

People thought being the Adventurers' Guild Master was a prestigious job. And Lars had to admit his office was nice. It took up the whole top floor of the guild, and everything was done in polished hardwood and shining bronze. He'd worked his way up to this position over fifteen years. It had been his goal since he joined the guild as a youthful archer intent on earning his way with his bow.

But now that he had his dream job, he found it a nightmare. It was true that he got to meet with the rich and powerful, but they didn't respect him. All they wanted were discounts on the guild's fees or introductions to other rich people that wanted discounts. They never got them of course. The guild had rules and even the guild master had to follow them. If he didn't, Lars would soon find himself looking for new employment. And the most important rule was that fees could only be waived in an emergency.

He sighed, sipped his expensive brandy and leaned back in his leather chair. No, losing all this, even if it wasn't what he thought it would be during his naive youth, didn't appeal to him at all.

A faint murmur reached him. A couple years ago, Lars had drilled a hole in the floor directly above Berend's office. His so-called assistant and a former alpha elite adventurer, Berend was the real power in the guild. Everyone respected him, unlike Lars, who most people sucked up to but truly disdained.

Ordinarily that wouldn't have bothered Lars, since it helped reduce his workload, but lately he'd been having doubts about his assistant's loyalty. Berend hadn't done anything overtly disloyal, but he had been meeting with some shady characters. Lars didn't know the whole story, but the bits and pieces he'd heard sounded bad.

Maybe his current guest would shine some light on the matter.

Lars tiptoed over to the listening hole and lay down beside it. The brief discussion grazed over some details mentioned in a letter Lars hadn't read. That wasn't ideal. When the guest—his name had come out a bit garbled but he was pretty sure it was Ronin—confirmed that he freed some beastfolk slaves and found gallons of plague cure potions, Lars's heart lurched. He'd heard of the potions, but never seen one. If the wizard this adventurer defeated was the source of the cure, that could be a problem.

The name Avius meant nothing to Lars. It sounded like a cover name. The sort of thing a wizard responsible for a plague might use.

The scrape of chairs made Lars flinch. He scrambled back from the listening hole and hurried over to his office door. He opened it a fraction and peered out in time to see a figure walking down the steps. Broad shoulders, shaved head, the scruffy shadow of a beard, and wearing sturdy leathers, he looked like any of a hundred adventurers Lars had met over the years. Nothing about Ronin struck him as remarkable.

Nevertheless, Lars needed to talk to him.

He waited until Ronin left the building, collected his heavy wool cloak, and hurried down the stairs and out the door. Trailing Ronin through the streets of Discourt wasn't that difficult given the lack of people on this bitterly cold evening. Lars shivered, thoughts of his half-finished brandy dancing in his head.

No! He had to focus. Ronin had no idea how dangerous Berend was. If he wasn't one of the man's loyal followers, he might be in danger.

Six blocks from the guild, Ronin crossed the street and climbed the stairs to an inn called The Day's End. It looked unremarkable, two stories, slate roof, just like a score of other inns in Discourt. It was the sort of place Lars wouldn't have given a second look most days. That might well be why Ronin chose it.

The door closed behind Ronin but Lars hesitated to follow. Berend had warned him against Lars. He knew his reputation wasn't the best while most people considered Berend a hero, mostly for putting up with him.

Steeling himself, Lars got ready to make his move. Before he could take a step, he sensed someone behind him. Turning, he reached for the dirk at his belt.

His heart skipped a beat when he found himself facing Berend. The former alpha elite adventurer was probably the strongest warrior in Discourt. Berend's expression was impassive, but Lars could sense the tightly coiled anger simmering under the surface.

"Out for a walk, Guild Master?"

"Yes, it gets so stuffy in my office. I thought a little brisk evening air would do me good."

"Of course. Still, it's a bit chilly for comfort," Berend said despite not showing any sign of discomfort. "Shall we walk back together?"

Lars looked over his shoulder at the inn. Despite phrasing it as a question, Lars knew an order when he heard one.

Turning back he said, "Sure, let's."

Berend clamped a hand on his shoulder, fingers like iron digging into the muscle through his heavy cloak. "Stay away from Ronin. That young man is mixed up in some dangerous matters and he doesn't need you getting in his way or confusing things."

"What sort of dangerous matters?" Lars asked.

"The sort that don't concern you. I'll handle everything to do with Ronin. You stay in your office, drink your brandy, and keep your mouth shut. Do that and everything will continue as it has. Do you understand?"

"Perfectly," Lars said.

With a final, painful squeeze Berend said, "I was confident you would. I just remembered another matter I need to attend to. I trust you can find your way back on your own."

"I'll manage. Good evening, Berend."

"Good evening, Guild Master."

The two men parted ways, with Berend turning down an alley to get up to who knew what sort of mischief. Lars felt certain that, whatever it was, it wouldn't be healthy for Ronin.

CHAPTER 23

I t felt like far too long since Danny had a comfortable bed and a warm room to sleep in. While far from a stranger to roughing it, sleeping on the ground or in the back of a wagon, especially in the winter, got old in a hurry. His room at The Day's End Inn was a perfect remedy for his weariness. The bed had a decent mattress and no bugs. His bowl of soup, steaming away on the nightstand, was filled with meat and vegetables. His mouth watered just thinking about it. He'd chosen the place at random, but it seemed he'd made a good call.

He grabbed his bowl and took a bite. The slightly spicy broth paired perfectly with the chunks of mutton. He could've eaten in the common room, but Danny had too much on his mind to enjoy the camaraderie.

First and foremost he had to admit that he was no closer to finding Avius than when he arrived. Granted, it had only been one day, but he'd had high hopes for his conversation with Berend. In the end, the assistant guild master hadn't told him much of use outside of his warning that the

Wizards' Guild was less than helpful when you were looking for a member. Assuming Avius was one.

Danny grabbed his satchel from its spot at the foot of the bed and pulled the letter Berend had written out. A wax seal with the guild's mark held the envelope shut. That was nothing a bit of fire magic couldn't solve. He melted the bottom of the seal just enough to pry it loose then popped the envelope open.

The letter was nothing special. It simply asked that every courtesy be extended to Danny as his investigation was of the utmost importance. There were no details about the search for Avius, which was probably a good idea on the off chance Danny lost the letter. The odds of that were long but not zero and Danny thoroughly approved of taking the cautious approach.

He was less certain what to think about Berend. He had a commanding presence, that was certain. If someone had told Danny he was the guild master, he would've believed it. In fact, if the current guy was such a mess, Danny didn't understand why he wasn't removed and Berend elevated. No doubt some politics were involved and Danny wanted nothing to do with it. He had plenty on his plate without poking the local authorities.

At least he could say without hesitation that saving Mother Ankie had been an unquestionable good. He was cautiously optimistic that the high priestess would be able to tell him something useful in the morning. At minimum, he'd be happy to hand off the cure potions to someone who could make use of them.

Danny polished off his soup and stood. No reason to make one of the serving girls come all the way up here just to collect his bowl. He could drop it off at the kitchen before hitting the sheets. The stress had caught up to him and Danny was exhausted.

He sealed his room with a spell and headed downstairs. The common room was half full, mostly with workers having dinner after a long day. Some of them looked rough but everyone was laughing and having a good time. It was a good vibe and Danny found himself smiling as he made his way to the kitchen door.

Five feet away it swung open and one of the serving girls emerged, running into him. She tripped and nearly fell. Thankfully her hands were empty and Danny caught her without making a mess.

"I'm sorry, are you okay?" he asked.

"Yes, thank you. The cook says I need to slow down going in and out, but I always forget. Are you finished? I can take your bowl for you."

"I appreciate it." Danny handed her the bowl and got a shy smile in return.

She ducked back into the kitchen and he turned for the stairs. Danny made it halfway across the common room before a beautiful woman with long blond hair and pale skin moved to intercept him. She wore a thin dress that only went down to midthigh and hugged her ample curves quite nicely. Her bright-green eyes glinted like emeralds.

Since he didn't believe in coincidences, Danny figured this was the same woman Mother Ankie healed. How she found him and what she wanted was another matter. One he was very keen to investigate.

"You were very sweet with that girl," she said.

"No reason not to be," Danny said. "Did you need something?"

She leaned forward and whispered, "Some company."

THE PLAGUE LANDS

Maybe his luck was turning around. It wasn't every day a man got propositioned by a beautiful assassin.

"I'm here alone. Would you like to come upstairs?"

"I thought you'd never ask." She reached for his hand and Danny quickly created a thin barrier of ether to keep their skin from touching. He had no idea how the assassin poisoned Mother Ankie and he wasn't going to take any chances.

He led the way upstairs. A few of the guys whistled as they went past, not that Danny blamed them given the beauty of his companion. Pity he doubted the evening was going to end the way they seemed to imagine.

An effort of will deactivated the ward he'd placed on the door and he pushed it open before stepping aside to let her go in first. He closed it, restored the ward, and added a sound-blocking aura. No one would be bothering them now.

"So were you looking for me specifically or was my treatment of the serving girl what caught your eye?" Danny asked.

She sat on the edge of the bed, her skirt riding up in a very distracting way. "Your kindness, of course. It's not like I've ever seen you before today. Perhaps you think me too forward."

"Not at all. Though I am impressed at how quickly you recovered from the plague. Mother Ankie's healing talents can't be underestimated."

Her gaze darted around the room as if seeking an escape route before returning to him. "I don't understand."

"Sure you do. After I eliminated whatever poison you gave her, she described you perfectly. Though I admit you're even more beautiful than I imagined. It's a shame you're a killer. Tonight might've been a lot more fun under different circumstances."

"Um…" She stood. "I think I'd like to go."

"I'll bet you would. Unfortunately, until you tell me who sent you to kill Mother Ankie and, I assume, me, you're not going anywhere."

"Someone help me!" she screamed at the top of her lungs. Her voice, so pleasant a moment ago, was now shrill with panic.

Danny waited a few seconds then said, "Doesn't look like anyone's coming. Do you want to scream some more or shall we have a proper chat? I'm not planning on hurting you. Not at the moment anyway. I just want to know who sent you."

She slumped in on herself. "I can't say."

"That's not going to cut it. Try again."

"It's the truth, I swear. There's some kind of spell on me that won't let me say who it is or anything about them."

Danny peered closer through the ether. There was no sign of psychic magic in her brain and he couldn't sense a lie. "Try and say his name."

"It won't work." Her voice trembled and she was on the verge of tears.

Ordinarily that sort of thing would trigger all sorts of protective feelings in him, but he had nothing to offer an assassin. "Humor me."

"My master's name is—" She fell silent midsentence. A spell of some sort flared to life, blocking a portion of her mind.

That confirmed she wasn't lying, which was both good and bad, though mostly bad. He could brute-force dispel the magic, but Danny wasn't sure how much damage he might do to her in the process. Why he cared about the fate of a killer was beyond him.

"Let's come at this from another direction," Danny said.

"Your arms, while quite shapely, aren't terribly muscular. How were you planning to kill me?"

"Poison, like I used on Mother Ankie. My master conducted an experiment on me and it made me immune to poison of any sort." She pointed at her bright-red lips. "My lip paint is toxic. One kiss and you'd be dead in an hour, though I would've made it a final hour to remember. Mother Ankie only lasted as long as she did thanks to the Goddess's blessing."

Danny could imagine worse ways to go, but even so he wasn't eager for that kiss. He used an ethereal tentacle to pull his satchel over to him and took out a scrap of cloth. "Here, clean that poison off. I don't want you to do something desperate and force me to kill you."

She wiped the lip paint and held out the cloth.

"Set it on the night stand for now."

She did as he said before hesitantly sitting on the edge of the bed. "What happens now?"

That was a damn good question. Shame he had no idea how to answer her. "Now I'm going to sleep. Stand up."

She did and Danny hit her with a full-power paralysis spell. Her body went rigid and he lowered her to the floor. That spell would hold her until he released it. "Sleep tight."

So saying he crawled into bed. Maybe Mother Ankie would have an idea how to clear the blocking spell out of her head. If not, Danny might have to risk damaging her to get the information he needed.

CHAPTER 24

D anny rubbed the crust from his eyes and looked down at the figure sprawled on the floor beside his bed. The beautiful assassin appeared to be sound asleep despite the paralysis spell holding her body rigid. Part of him had hoped the previous night's events had been a bad dream, but it seemed he was doomed to disappointment.

Light streamed through the window, which should mean someone was awake and active at the Goddess's temple. Mother Ankie was the strongest magic user he felt confident was on his side. Hopefully she could help him remove the psychic block that prevented the assassin from talking. Danny got the feeling after their brief chat last night that the woman wouldn't hesitate to turn on her master if she had the ability.

There was nothing like being used as a guinea pig in a magical experiment to make you dislike someone.

"Hey." Danny nudged her with his right foot.

She let out a groan and opened her eyes. And that was all

she could move without his permission. Danny figured if she could kill him using nothing but her eyelashes, he deserved to die.

"Time to wake up," Danny said. "I'm going to let you move, but I'm adding a death spell that will disintegrate you in an instant should you try anything."

"I'm not going to try anything," she said. "I spent a lot of time thinking last night and I decided you're my best chance of getting free of my master. I'll do whatever I can within the bounds of my binding."

"How does he control you?" Danny swung his legs off the bed and pulled his socks and boots on. "Stopping you from talking is fairly simple, but forcing you to kill someone is a whole other thing."

"I don't know how it works, only that I have to do whatever the masked man says. The compulsion isn't limitless. For example, my need to kill you vanished late last night. My best guess is it only lasts twelve hours. I've never had a task last longer than that."

Danny, or more accurately his host body, had no knowledge of such a spell. Which meant absolutely nothing given his focus on combat magic. Danny could blow stuff up with the best of them, but the subtle uses of magic remained largely a mystery to him.

"We're going to see if we can do something about that today. Mother Ankie should be able to remove the spell. And if she can't, I'll do it and she can heal your brain should I break something."

"I'm not fond of the way you put that. More importantly, are you sure they won't cut me down the moment I arrive at the temple? I did try and kill the high priestess."

"Worshippers of the Goddess don't work that way. Now,

if you'd tried to kill the high priest of the Binder, I'd be more concerned for your long-term health."

She laughed before realizing what she'd done and making a face. "This isn't how I thought my morning was going to go."

"No? How did you think it was going to go?"

"I figured you'd kill me and find some way to dispose of my body."

"Well, it's still early. I'm going to step out into the hall so you can have a bit of privacy. When you're done, knock once."

Fifteen minutes later, they were both as ready as they were going to be. Danny held out his hand. "Hold on and don't let go. I'm going to make us invisible. If your masked master is watching the inn, I don't want him spotting us and knowing for sure his plan failed."

She hesitated before slipping her delicate hand in his. Danny didn't know what she did before ending up in her current predicament, but nothing about her screamed assassin. He had no idea if he'd be able to help her escape her master, but he was determined to do his best.

He activated his stealth field and willed it to expand to her as well. Once they were both invisible and silent, he led the way down to the common room. They had a decent crowd and the smell of fresh bread and bacon made his mouth water. But food would have to wait.

They stood beside the door and the next time it opened slipped out into the chilly streets. Since she didn't have a cloak of her own, Danny slung his partway around her. He didn't know if it would do much good, but hopefully his body heat would help keep her a little warmer.

They moved like ghosts through Discourt, ignoring the

sights and smells, unnoticed by the people hurrying through the streets on their errands. He wasn't sure he'd ever get used to the stealth field's power.

At last they reached the temple district. When he was confident no one was around to see, he ended the spell. They quick marched the last few yards to the Goddess's temple and Danny gratefully pushed through the door into the nice, warm entry area.

A different priestess was behind the counter this morning. She looked from Danny to the assassin and back. Her eyes widened all of a sudden. "Would you be Mr. Ronin?"

"Yes, ma'am. I'd like to speak with Mother Ankie if she's awake. It's a matter of some urgency."

"I don't know if she's up yet. Only Father Koen visits her regularly. I was supposed to let you in whenever you showed up, but I'd hate to wake her..." The priestess seemed totally at a loss as to what she should do.

"Why don't you get Father Koen and he can tell us?"

She brightened. "Good idea. He's usually in the chapel praying at this time of day. Wait here while I check."

The priestess hurried through the door, leaving Danny and the assassin alone.

"You can let my hand go," she said. "I'm not going to run away. Whatever punishment fate has in store for me I've earned many times over."

Danny hadn't even realized he was still holding her hand and let go at once. "I think you'll be pleasantly surprised by Mother Ankie. She didn't strike me as the vengeful sort."

The priestess quickly returned, this time with Father Koen. The priest only glanced at Danny for a moment then stared at the assassin. A perfectly reasonable reaction to such a beautiful woman. Though Danny had his doubts it was her killer body that got his attention.

"Is she the one who poisoned Mother Ankie?" When Danny nodded, his jaw dropped. "Why, in the Goddess's name, did you bring her here?"

"She's got a spell on her keeping her from telling me about her master. I need Mother Ankie's help removing it. Don't worry, the compulsion that forced her to try and kill the high priestess has long since expired. It'll be perfectly safe."

"No! Under no circumstance will I allow that woman into Ankie's presence. Even if she behaves, who knows what sort of psychological damage seeing her would-be killer might cause."

Danny scrubbed his hand across his face. "Do you really think she's that mentally weak?"

Father Koen's jaw bunched as he grimaced. He couldn't very well admit that he thought the temple's high priestess was mentally weak. But if he couldn't do that, his main reason for stopping Danny went out the window.

At last, he said, "Fine, I'll ask her. But if Ankie doesn't want to talk to her, that's the end of it."

"Agreed. The sooner we do this the better."

Father Koen stalked off toward Mother Ankie's room without another word. Danny and the assassin fell in behind him. When Danny caught her looking at him, he winked. Why he was trying to make the woman feel better he wasn't totally sure. Maybe because she was as much a victim as the people she'd been forced to kill. She didn't strike him as evil, just sad.

A different set of guards was on duty when they arrived and one of them opened the door for Father Koen and said,

"She finished her breakfast a few minutes ago and mentioned a desire to take a walk later."

Father Koen nodded and went inside. The update sounded like good news to Danny. A hungry patient who wanted to get out of bed meant they were on the mend.

The meeting didn't take long and a couple minutes after he entered, Father Koen returned, looking even grumpier than when he entered. "Mother Ankie has agreed to see you."

That explained his bad mood. The priest ushered them in. The high priestess sat propped up by a handful of pillows in her bed, looking much less like a woman on death's doorstep. Her cheeks, while still a bit sunken, had good color and she favored him with a bright smile.

When her gaze shifted to the assassin the smile faded. "Come closer, young lady."

The assassin hesitated then took a step. She moved as if through water, every stride painfully slow. Danny was ready to activate his slaying spell at the first sign of her trying anything. Beside him, Father Koen looked on the verge of an aneurysm. Danny didn't know if priests got drunk, but after this, he wouldn't be surprised if the good father hit the sauce.

"Tell me what happened," Mother Ankie said.

"She can't," Danny said. "That's why we're here."

He filled her in on everything that happened after he left the temple. "I was hoping you could remove the psychic block. I can do it if I have to, but my talents lie in brute-force magic. I fear I might hurt her."

Father Koen snorted. "She's an assassin. Who cares if you hurt her?"

"Father Koen!" Mother Ankie said, her tone as sharp as Danny had heard it. "This poor girl is a victim. Where's your compassion? As a priest of the Goddess, you should be ashamed of yourself. I certainly am."

"Ankie…" Father Koen couldn't have sounded more hurt if Danny had stabbed him with the ethersword.

Mother Ankie patted the assassin's hand. "Don't worry, dear, we'll get you straightened out by the Goddess's grace. Sit beside me."

She eased down beside Mother Ankie and perched on the edge of the bed as if she were a bird ready to take flight at any moment.

The high priestess peered at her head, a little frown creasing her lips. "This is remarkable work. Picking it out will be no easy thing. Ronin, you will have to help me."

"I'm happy to do what I can, but as I said, this sort of delicate work isn't my forte."

"Don't worry, all I need you to do is disperse the ether as I work the tendrils out of her brain. If you don't, I fear they might imbed themselves again elsewhere."

"I can handle that. Are you ready?" His question was directed as much at the assassin as Mother Ankie.

"Let's begin," Mother Ankie said.

It wasn't a speedy process. Inch by inch Mother Ankie picked the fine threads of ether out of the assassin's mind. As soon as she did, Danny blasted them into sparkling motes. He couldn't have said how long the process took, but eventually the final speck of ether came free and he blew it away.

A shudder ran through the assassin and she slumped in place.

"Is she okay?" Danny asked.

Mother Ankie touched her with a glowing hand and the assassin perked up. Her bright-green eyes focused on Danny. "My name is Melina. Thank you both for setting me free."

Danny grinned. "You're perfectly welcome. I've got a lot of questions, but what do you think about something to eat first?"

Melina gave an eager nod. "I'm starving."

"I could eat as well," Mother Ankie said. "Channeling that much of the Goddess's power always leaves me ravenous. Father Koen, be a good fellow and see what the kitchen can whip up."

Father Koen looked pained at being dismissed. Though to be fair he pretty much always looked pained about something.

When he'd gone Melina said, "I don't think he likes me. Not that I blame him."

"It's his nature," Mother Ankie said. "I'm generally far too easy on people. Father Koen balances me with his sternness. We're a good team, but sometimes he lets his nature get the best of him. He also tends to be overprotective of me. While I appreciate all he does, it gets annoying."

"How did you end up with Avius anyway?" Danny didn't know how long the food would take to arrive so he figured a couple quick questions wouldn't hurt anything.

"Is that the wizard's name? He bought me at the northern slave market. I was thirteen at the time. He kept me in his lab for three years, conducting experiments and casting control spells. I never got the impression the results were what he wanted, though when he finally confirmed that I was immune to poison, he seemed pleased."

"Slavery isn't legal in the Five Kingdoms," Danny said. "Is it common around here?"

"Not right around here," Mother Ankie said. "Discourt has no slave market, and though there's no law against slavery, it is frowned upon by the rich and powerful. The northern clans, on the other hand, have a strong tradition of slave trading. They raid each other constantly as well as coming to the plains to capture beastfolk. Sometimes they'll hit a small village, burn it to the ground, and take anyone they can back to sell. It's a disgusting practice and the temples argue against it as much as possible. Except the Binder's, who consider it acceptable in certain situations."

"I'm surprised the wealthy look down on slavery."

Mother Ankie snorted. "It's not because of any noble sentiment. Having paid servants acts as a way for them to display how rich they are. Having slaves is the same as admitting you're too poor to pay your help."

"I never thought about it that way." Danny looked around. "Going to be hard eating standing up. You don't have any chairs for guests?"

"Of course I do. I just prefer to keep them out of sight." Mother Ankie concentrated and the white disk of a pocket dimension opened. "Could you bring the table and chairs out?"

Danny walked around and looked inside. The space was way smaller than his, about the size of a modest walk-in closet, but it was still plenty to store a round table and four chairs. He pulled everything out and set them up in the open space beside her bed. While he doubted Father Koen would want to join them, setting a place for him was the polite thing to do.

Father Koen returned not long after and they enjoyed a late breakfast. When all that remained were cups of tea Mother Ankie said, "Now, let us share stories. I have little to tell, myself. The plague hasn't been a major issue for Discourt. I think I've healed twenty people altogether."

"I've turned aside three parties while on gate duty," Father

Koen said. "Considering the traffic we see during better weather, that's hardly worth mentioning."

Danny went next, telling them everything he'd seen since leaving Fell Forest. When he finished, he opened his storage and pulled out one of the kegs of cure potion. "We were hoping the temple would be willing to handle distribution of the cure, but if there aren't many sick people in the city, that might not be the best idea."

"We can work together with the other temples and arrange a healing caravan," Mother Ankie said. "It will travel from village to village, helping as many people as possible."

Danny had never heard of such a thing, but it sounded like a good idea. He put the cure potion back in storage for now and turned to Melina. "What can you tell us about Avius?"

"Not a lot, I'm afraid. He didn't really talk to me. I was just a research subject to him, not a person. I'm not even sure where his lab is. When he sent me here, he brought me out blindfolded."

Danny had been hoping for better news. "What about the masked man?"

She shook her head. "He only speaks to me to issue orders. I live in a small apartment in the residential district. I assume he pays for it since no one has ever asked me for rent. He also provides a small stipend to cover my expenses. It isn't much, but I'm in no danger of starving. At least I wasn't. Returning to my place seems unwise now. I'm not sure what I'm going to do."

"You can stay here," Mother Ankie said. "We have plenty of rooms. There's always something that needs doing. You can help out in exchange for room and board."

"Thank you," Melina said. "I'll try my best to be worthy of your kindness."

Mother Ankie patted her hand. "Kindness is its own reward, dear. We who follow the Goddess live to serve others."

"What's your address?" Danny asked. "I'll swing by and pick up your stuff."

Melina's eyes widened. "It could be dangerous. The masked man might be there."

Danny's smile had an edge to it. "I dearly hope he is. It would make my life so much easier."

CHAPTER 25

The walk from the Goddess's temple to Discourt's low-income residential district took Danny about twenty minutes. The neighborhood didn't look dangerous so much as worn out. It was a labyrinth of weathered buildings and small shops built practically on top of each other. In some places they were packed so closely together the sun could barely make it to the ground. Those spots reminded him of Fell Forest, thankfully minus the aura of corruption.

Finding a specific address was no easy task, but eventually he reached Melina's apartment building. Its exterior needed a paint job and the three steps leading to the front door looked like they'd been attacked by rats. The masked man, whoever he was, didn't keep his assassin in style, that was certain.

He took the steps in one stride and pushed through the door. There was an empty foyer with a hall leading deeper into the building. Melina's place was on the second floor so he headed for the stairs at the end of the hall. They were in better shape than the ones out front and didn't even creak as he climbed them.

On the second-floor landing he paused. The silence was creepy. People lived here, he could sense a few of their life forces. His optimistic theory was they worked nights and were sleeping.

Whatever their situation, it was none of his business. Danny had too much on his plate already.

He quickly located apartment twenty-three. Of course the door was locked and Melina didn't have a key, only the masked man did. She said he gave it back to her after she completed her mission and met him at the designated place. So much time had passed she assured him he'd be long gone. Well, a locked door was no obstacle to Danny and a little ethereal manipulation soon had the lock undone.

He nudged the door open and stepped inside. The only light came from a small window that looked out over an alley. Not the greatest of views. The apartment itself was as empty as Mother Ankie's. A bed was shoved against one wall, a nightstand with a single drawer beside it, and a trunk at the foot. No decorations brightened the place up. Just the bare essentials for existence.

Looked like a miserable way to live. Not that Danny was one to talk. He didn't even have a home.

Right, focus. He moved to the footlocker and flipped the lid open to reveal its contents. Three dresses, one simple and two sexy, like the one she wore to seduce him last night. Those had to be for work. Beside them was a pair of sturdy shoes, the leather scuffed from years of wear. Danny's fingers brushed against a small homemade doll, its yarn hair tangled and the button eyes staring up at him. It was the only thing out of place and he couldn't imagine its purpose. Maybe it didn't have any beyond being something for her to hug at night.

He gathered everything and placed them into his storage. One last look around confirmed there was nothing else to take.

Satisfied he had everything and disappointed that the masked man hadn't put in an appearance, Danny left the apartment, locking it up again with his magic. He didn't know why he bothered; there was nothing left to steal.

The walk back to the exit was every bit as silent as the walk up, but that ended the moment he stepped out into the street. Someone shouted from his right and he caught the sound of a scuffle. It was none of his business, but curiosity got the better of him.

He ran down the street to a narrow alley where a young man about the same age as Danny's host body was trying to pull away from a pair of black-armored soldiers who were in turn trying to drag him out the opposite end of the alley.

Looked like Danny's luck was improving.

"Hey!" he shouted. "Leave him alone!"

One of the soldiers turned Danny's way. His black-lacquered helmet had a mask built in that covered the top of his face. "Best mind your own business, stranger. We're taking this one in on the lord mayor's order."

Danny nodded. "Okay. I'll come along with you. If you're going to turn him over to the proper authorities there shouldn't be a problem, right?"

The guard growled. "You should've taken the hint."

He drew his sword and stalked toward Danny.

Any concern Danny might've had about these two really working for the lord mayor vanished. No way would anyone with legitimate authority attack a random passerby asking reasonable questions.

Danny drew his own sword and met the soldier halfway. Three quick blows confirmed the man knew his business but was no match for Danny.

Then his partner came running in.

The two of them working together didn't amount to much either. Danny increased the power to his physical enhancements and ended the fight with a fist to the first man's temple and a side kick that sent the second crashing into the wall of the nearby building.

"Don't worry, kid, it's o—" Danny turned to find the youth they were trying to arrest long gone. "—kay. That's a fine thank-you."

Maybe these clowns could tell him something useful. Danny kicked the man he punched over on his back. A small burst of healing magic brought him around. When he saw Danny's sword at his throat his eyes got wide.

"From your expression I see you understand your circumstances. Where were you taking him?"

The soldier's mouth opened, but before he could utter a word the ether surged in his brain. A moment later his head exploded.

Danny grimaced. That was a first.

Lucky he had a spare prisoner to interrogate.

As soon as he thought it the second guy's head exploded.

He spun around, searching for whoever triggered the magic. There had to be a wizard around here somewhere. He hadn't even spoken to the second guy, so that didn't set the spell off.

There were life forces all around, but it was impossible to say which, if any, was responsible. The killer could be any of them or he could be watching through a crystal ball like the one Danny took from Osbern.

"Well, shit," he muttered. "Another dead end."

With nothing better to do, he turned back toward the temple.

The walk was peaceful and soon the familiar outline of the Goddess's temple appeared ahead. Danny went in and, after a quick nod to the priestess on duty, headed right to Mother Ankie's room.

"Back already? That was quick." The guard on duty knocked on her door. "Ronin's here."

"Let him in, please."

The guard opened the door and Danny went in. He found the high priestess still in bed, sitting up with a book in her lap. She looked even more recovered than when he left and that was only an hour or so ago. It had to be the Goddess's blessing at work.

"Mother Ankie. I thought I might find Melina with you. I've got her stuff."

"Father Koen is getting her settled." Her eyes crinkled. "Did you have trouble? You look anxious."

Danny told her about the soldiers. "Does the lord mayor have his own private troops?"

"Not that I know of. He is rich and powerful, so he might have some private guards that serve him, but the guards answer to the city council as a whole. I can say for sure he's no wizard."

"Which means he didn't put the spell that killed them in their heads. Bet I know who did."

"I suspect we both do. What will you do now?"

"I still need to visit the Wizards' Guild, but first I'll give

Melina her stuff. Hopefully it'll make her new place feel a bit more like home."

"She's in the priests' dormitory," Mother Ankie said. "Go through the infirmary, out the rear door, and take a right. I'm not sure which room, but you shouldn't have any trouble tracking her down from there."

"Thanks. If I learn anything interesting I'll be in touch."

Danny left her room behind and made his way to the dormitory. The infirmary was mostly unoccupied. Two patients, both of them older folks, were sleeping in neighboring beds. Danny had no idea what was wrong with them, but was confident his magic would keep him safe.

Once he reached the dormitory he spotted Father Koen standing in the hall about halfway down the passage. That was convenient. Danny strode his way. As soon as the priest noticed him he winced which brought a grin to Danny's face. It seemed Father Koen didn't have a good opinion of him. Probably afraid he was going to bring more trouble.

"Morning, Father," Danny said. "I've got Melina's things. Could you direct me to her room?"

Melina's head popped out of the doorway directly across from Father Koen. "Ronin! Welcome back. Did you have any trouble?"

Danny debating about telling her what happened, but in the end saw no reason to keep it a secret. "I didn't see the masked man you warned me about, but I did run into some black-armored soldiers who were trying to kidnap a young man. I stopped them but before I could question them, someone caused their heads to explode. The kid they were after left before I had a chance to ask him any questions."

"How horrific," Father Koen said.

"Messy too," Danny said. "You don't happen to know who the soldiers work for, do you?"

Melina shook her head. "Neither Master Avius nor the masked man told me anything I didn't absolutely need to know for a mission. I'm sure they had many secrets I knew nothing about."

He hadn't been overly optimistic that Melina would know anything, but having her confirm it was still disappointing. "Can I come in? I've got your stuff."

"Of course." She moved aside to let him through.

The room they provided Melina was nicer than her little apartment. Everything was clean and freshly painted. The sheets looked like they'd just been washed, and the faint scent of flowers filled the air.

Danny opened his storage, took out her dresses and laid them carefully on the bed, set her shoes on the floor in front of it, and finally held out the little doll. "I was surprised to find this."

"Master Avius gave it to me not long after he bought me." Melina took the doll, a conflicted look on her face. "I cried constantly when I first arrived at the lab. I think this was his attempt to make me feel better. It was the only kind thing he ever did for me. I hate him, yet can't bring myself to throw it away. Is that strange?"

As Danny debated how to reply, he peered more closely at the doll through the ether. As far as he could tell, there was no magic attached to it. It was just a normal doll.

At last he said, "I think you're attached to it more because it helped you through a hard time than because of who gave it to you. I wouldn't worry."

Her smile held a certain warmth that made her even more beautiful. "Thanks."

"Do you need anything else?"

"No, I'm good. Besides, you've already given me too much as it is."

"Okay. I'll check in on you again later. Take care." Before he could leave she darted in and kissed him on the cheek. "What was that for?"

"Just because."

Danny wasn't sure how to respond, so he just nodded and took his leave. Father Koen had already made himself scarce so Danny retraced his steps through the temple. He'd been hoping to run into Michael. He and the young priest hadn't discussed their long-term plans, but Danny assumed he had to get back to Redfield. Since he had no idea how long this investigation was going to take, Danny wanted to make arrangements should Michael wish to return.

Well, maybe the temple could handle it. For now, Danny had some wizards to chat with.

CHAPTER 26

Berend stood, wrapped in his heaviest cloak, across the street from The Day's End Inn not far from where he confronted Lars the day before. The sun had barely risen but he wanted to be here early lest he miss something. He'd sent Melina to kill Ronin last night. The man was poking his nose into places it didn't belong and if it kept up, he was bound to learn things Berend wanted kept secret.

The beautiful assassin had never failed him before. He didn't count the high priestess of the Goddess surviving as a failure. Melina had poisoned the woman exactly as she was supposed to. An archangel's blessing wasn't something you could plan for. She'd been taken out of play and the city had begun to second-guess Heaven's blessings. It was close enough to total victory for him.

Unlike Mother Ankie, Ronin was nothing, an ordinary adventurer barely risen to elite status. One kiss and he should've been dead in short order. And who could resist a kiss from Melina?

He sighed. When she didn't return to report her success last night, he knew something must have gone wrong. What it might be Berend had no idea. Thus his early morning visit to the inn.

The day stretched on as people came and went but neither of the people he actually wanted to see appeared. By the time midmorning rolled around he was losing his patience. Walking in and asking about Ronin wouldn't work. Innkeepers were notorious for sharing nothing about their guests. Their business required discretion. An innkeeper who got a reputation for talking wouldn't be open for long. And in Discourt, if they talked about the wrong person, they might not be breathing for long either.

His scowl deepened as he turned away from the inn. He'd wasted as much time as he could. Maybe Avius could tell him something useful. Melina had been his test subject for years; he had to have some way to find her.

Berend left the working-class neighborhood behind and headed for home. He lived in the merchant district. It was full of nice houses and people who would cut your throat for a silver coin. Plenty of people said adventurers were only in it for the gold. Whenever anyone said it they made the idea sound like a bad thing. Everyone was in it for the gold. What did they think, that adventurers risked their lives for fun?

He turned down a white cobblestone street. He lived on the edge of the district. Despite his many successes before he took a job with the guild, Berend could afford nothing better. His house had two stories and a wrought iron fence topped with spikes. He passed through the gate, unlocked the door, and stepped inside. Berend lived alone and his bachelor preferences were clear in the lack of decorations and furniture. He had what he needed and nothing more.

Leaving the foyer behind, he turned down a hall to the kitchen. At the back of the larder he reached under a shelf and unlocked a hidden door. Pushing through, he entered a simple room with a desk, chair, and coat rack. The rack held a dark cloak and mask, the disguise of his alter ego and the only face Melina would recognize. His gaze shifted, settling on the crystal ball sitting atop the desk. Much as he hated talking to the wizard, he needed to know what was going on.

Berend sat in his chair and rested his fingers on the cool crystal. "Avius."

A vibration ran through the crystal as it sent out a signal to a matching crystal. Now it was a waiting game. If the wizard was busy with something he might not reply for hours. Though such a long delay was rare.

Today he only needed ten minutes, which was quick for Avius. Darkness filled the crystal and when it parted, Avius's scarred face appeared.

"Berend, to what do I owe this dubious pleasure?"

"Melina's gone missing. I sent her to eliminate the adventurer who's been digging into our business. She didn't return and now I can't find her. Do you have some magical means of locating her?"

"I could use a scrying spell," Avius said. "Did she truly fail to kill this man?"

"I'm not certain, but given what I know so far, I have to say yes."

"Remarkable. So far Ronin has defeated a number of my mercenaries, thwarted Osbern's effort to sell the potion in the east, and now he's defeated your assassin. You said he was nothing but an ordinary adventurer. Do you stand by your assessment?"

"I have no information to suggest otherwise. If he's a day

over seventeen I'll eat one of those stupid wolves your apprentice likes so much. It has to be luck."

"Hmm. Lucky or not, he needs to go. Wait a moment while I try to find Melina." The crystal went all black.

Berend clenched his fist until the knuckles turned white. Everything had been going so well. Now this Ronin shows up and it all starts falling apart. Berend had invested too much time and effort to lose everything now.

Half an hour passed in the silent room before Avius finally reappeared in the crystal. "She is hidden from me. Wherever Melina's gone, it's powerfully warded against scrying. That means one of the temples or the Wizards' Guild most likely. She needs to be recovered and Ronin killed. Surely that's not too great a task for a former alpha elite adventurer."

"No, I will deal with him," Berend said. "Ronin trusts me. He thinks I'm the only honest man at the guild. That will give me an advantage. May I use some of the mercenaries?"

"By all means. The sooner this is dealt with the better."

"What about Ronin's whereabouts? Can you find him?"

"No. He's insufficiently familiar to me for scrying." Something caused Avius to look away from the crystal. When he turned back he said, "Something has come up. Deal with this adventurer, Berend. He could ruin everything."

The crystal died, leaving Berend alone in his hidden room. He stood in the dark, thinking. Melina was likely at one of the temples. Ronin mentioned being on good terms with the Goddess's temple. Assuming he captured her, that was the most probable place. The Wizards' Guild made no sense given his lack of connections there.

Berend's eyes widened and he snapped his fingers. Ronin

said he planned to visit the guild today. That would be the perfect place to make contact.

He hurried out of the hidden room, a plan already forming as he went. He threw his cloak back on and strode into the cold.

Berend had lived in Discourt his entire life and navigated the back streets with ease. From his home, it was only a ten-minute walk to the Wizards' Guild. When he reached the gray stone tower he paused. It would be for the best to meet Ronin outside. Show a bit of desperation and a bit of worry over a new friend.

He could imagine the conversation already. Cast a bit more doubt on the guild master. A nudge here and suggestion there and soon he'd know where to find Melina and how best to kill Ronin.

CHAPTER 27

D anny spotted the Wizards' Guild from a fair
distance. The square stone tower rose well above
every other building in the area. It was certainly a
far cry from the simple storefront the guild worked out of in
Villipan City. Mother Ankie warned him the guild was
unlikely to hand out any information about a member,
assuming Avius was a member. Danny had no doubt she was
right, but on the other hand, pointing out that one of their
members was a kidnapper, slave owner, and the cause of the
plague might loosen a few tongues.

At least, he hoped it would. If he struck out here, Danny
wasn't sure what his next move might be.

He rounded the corner to the front of the building. There
were no guards on duty, which didn't surprise him. Most
people were nervous around wizards. You'd have to be a
little crazy to try and steal from their guild.

As he approached, someone came jogging his way from
across the street. Danny paused and frowned. He knew next
to no one in this city and most of them were at the temple.

The stranger's hooded wool cloak cast shadows over his face.

A few paces away he waved. "Ronin! I've been worried about you."

"Berend? Why are you here and why were you worried about me?"

"After you left yesterday, I spotted the guild master following you. I trailed him to your inn. Despite warning him off, I feared he might have tried something."

That made no sense. If Berend had been worried, he should've come in and said something to Danny. Like, "Hey, the sketchy guild master knows where you're staying, keep your wits about you." Since he didn't, Danny went on guard at once.

He activated a lie detecting spell and said, "I appreciate your concern, but as you can see, everything's fine. Was there anything else?"

Berend stared for a moment as if expecting Danny to say something else. "Not right now. I've put out some inquiries to my old adventuring buddies. Hopefully some of them will be able to give me some information on Avius."

Well, that was one steaming pile of bullshit. Any faith Danny had in Berend withered and blew away. He was starting to think the much-maligned guild master might be worth talking to after all.

"Hopefully," Danny said. "The guy's a tough one to pin down. I don't know if the guild will have any information, but I'll find out soon enough."

"If I learn anything should I send a message to your inn?"

"That's fine, thanks. See you later."

Danny left the lying assistant guild master and marched up to the Wizards' Guild's front door. It was a heavy-duty thing painted black and featuring a demon-head door knocker. Subtle was not the word Danny would've used to describe it.

Well, whatever. He slammed the knocker down a couple times and waited.

Only a few seconds later a young woman in a gray robe the same color as the tower opened the door. "Can I help you, sir?"

"I wanted to talk to someone about a wizard who calls himself Avius. I'm trying to find him."

"Are you a member?"

"No, is that a problem?"

"The guild master only speaks with members and he's the only one that could tell you something like that."

"Okay, what do I need to do to join?" Danny asked.

She flinched, clearly taken aback by his question. "Um, you need to be able to do magic and pay the five-gold-piece membership fee. That's annual, not lifetime."

"No problem." Danny raised his hand and conjured a ball of fire over it. He let it float there for a second before banishing it. Then he reached into his satchel and pulled out five of his new gold coins. "Here you go. Do I get a badge or something?"

"Yeah, maybe you should come in. I don't usually handle new registrations on the front porch."

"I can see where that would be inefficient." Danny motioned her back into the tower.

Taking the hint, she backed up and he followed her inside. There was a little greeting area right beyond the door with a long bar stopping anyone from going deeper into the building. A three-foot section had been raised and she slipped through the gap and lowered it again.

She reached under the bar and pulled out a sheet of paper, a quill, and a pot of ink. "Okay, let's do this properly. Name?"

"Ronin," Danny said. He figured it would be best to register under the same name as the one he used at the Adventurers' Guild.

"Is that your real name or a pseudonym?"

"Does it matter?"

"Not really. A lot of wizards use pseudonyms since there's a school of magic that can use your true name to render you weak to the magic of a person who knows it. It's a very rare and time consuming sort of magic, but it does exist."

"Good to know. What's the next question?"

"Right. What's your magical specialty?"

"I'm an arcane knight, so physical enhancement and combat-related spells."

She brightened as she jotted down his answer. "That explains it. When I saw you I assumed you were a warrior. We don't have many arcane knights joining the guild. They tend to be disinterested in research and the more complex uses of magic. No offense."

"None taken. I'm only joining because I want to speak with the guild master about Avius. I'm treating the five gold pieces like a bribe to get in."

"That's rather blunt. You could at least pretend to be excited about joining."

"I'm bad at pretending. Do you have any more questions?"

She asked a couple more, mostly about whether he planned to open a magic shop and what he planned to sell.

"Okay, that's all," she said. "Here are the rules. You can't share any information you find in our library with nonmembers. You also can't take any of the books out of the tower. As a member you're entitled to a twenty percent discount at any guild-associated magic shop as well as on services we offer here at the tower. Any questions?"

"Do I get a badge or something?"

"Sure do. I'll get it ready for you. But first I'll see if the guild master is free to speak with you. Wait here, please."

"Thanks." The girl took his gold and strode off deeper into the tower. If she ever got dragged to Earth, she'd have a great future working at the DMV. What a bunch of rigamarole just to talk to someone.

They didn't even have any chairs in the waiting area. He didn't know if it was some sort of power play or if they were just jerks. He settled for leaning against the counter. Hopefully she wouldn't be too long.

After a tedious half hour, the receptionist returned. She handed him a silver disk about the size of his palm. It featured a book and a wand on the front, and had his name on the back. "Here's your badge. The guild master is free and looking forward to meeting you."

That last bit triggered his lie detecting spell, but Danny saw no need to point it out. "Great. Where are we meeting?"

"The consultation room." She lifted the section of bar out of the way. "Follow me."

Danny put the badge in his satchel and followed her back into the tower. The walls were bare save for white crystals set at regular intervals which provided a pleasant, even light.

They passed two doors before she stopped and pushed the third one open. "He'll be along shortly."

"Where do you have the classes for prospective wizards?"

"Second floor. The whole thing is dedicated to teaching those with potential."

Danny nodded and entered the consultation room. It was nothing impressive, but at least there were chairs around the table. Hard, wooden chairs, granted, but you could sit on them. And he did, taking the chair facing the door. The other three walls were blank, but just to be safe, Danny placed a ward around himself. If there was a secret door, he wouldn't be taken by surprise.

Thankfully his wait was a short one. After a few minutes the door opened and an elegant man dressed in a gray robe identical to the one worn by the secretary entered. Danny put his age at midforties based on the amount of gray in his goatee.

Danny hopped to his feet, canceled his ward, and stuck out his hand. "Guild Master?"

"Thaddeus." The man gave him a limp handshake. "You would be Mr. Ronin, our newest member. You wished to speak with me about someone named Avius, correct?"

"That's right. I assumed he was a member since this crazy wizard I fought claimed he was plucked out of your magic class by Avius and made his apprentice."

Thaddeus gestured at the table. "Perhaps you should tell me everything."

Danny sat back down and laid out an edited version of the last few weeks. "So as best I can tell, Avius is the source of the plague. Why anyone would want to release a plague is beyond me and it doesn't matter anyway. I just need to find him and stop him."

"I can't tell if you are a complete, raving lunatic or the best liar I've ever met. Are you using anti-psychic magic? Something is blocking my lie detection spell."

"I keep an anti-psychic magic spell active at all times. I

had the misfortune to run into a succubus this summer and her magic gave me all sorts of problems. As for the story, I assure you it's the truth. Feel free to confirm it with Mother Ankie at the Goddess's temple."

"I've never gotten along with priests. Assuming you're telling me the truth, not a fact I'm willing to accept yet, there are a few problems. The first and most obvious being the plague is already out in the population. Even if you find and kill this wizard, it will change nothing."

"You might be right, but, assuming Avius created the plague, he might have notes detailing the process. My main hope is that I can find something to let the priests heal it more easily. The disease is terrifyingly resistant to magical healing. And even if I find nothing of use, at a bare minimum, a dead wizard isn't going to create another plague should this one fail to achieve the results he wants. What were your other problems?"

"For one thing, we do not now nor have we ever had a member named Avius."

"I didn't think it was his real name. What about someone taking one of your students as an apprentice?" Danny described the wizard he fought. "It would've been a few years ago. Ring any bells?"

Thaddeus stared off into space as if lost in his own little world. Danny was tempted to wave his hand in front of the man's face but resisted.

After a couple minutes of silence he said, "In fact, one of our students was hired by a man by the name of Lord Carbey. He said his house wizard needed an assistant and asked for our most promising student."

Thaddeus hadn't told a single lie so far, but there was a

lot wrong with what he just said. "I didn't think this area had nobles."

"We don't call them nobles, but we do have a number of exceedingly wealthy families that control large tracts of land and employ soldiers. They have no authority to make laws or levy taxes, but in every other way they'd pass for nobility."

"Interesting. So how did this nobleman who isn't a noble get into the guild without being a member?"

"He made a very generous donation to the guild to help pay for our school."

Danny was shocked—shocked!— to discover a sufficient quantity of money was all it took for someone to overlook their rules. More importantly, it sounded like this guy's house wizard was Avius.

"Where can I find him?" Danny asked.

Thaddeus looked pained, the first emotion other than contempt Danny had seen flit across his features. "I would ask that you not trouble our wealthiest patron. It'll cause trouble for the guild."

Danny stood. "Your patron may be harboring a mass murderer. How's that going to make the guild look? Listen, if this house wizard isn't Avius, I'll apologize for bothering him and move on, but if it is, Lord Carbey might be in trouble. Think how generous he'd be if I rescued him from a crazed wizard."

Fear and greed warred on Thaddeus's face. At last he said, "You wouldn't drop this even if I ordered you to, right?"

"No chance," Danny agreed.

"Fine. I've told you all I intend to. However you go about finding Lord Carbey's estate, it won't be from me."

"Fair enough. Thanks for the information, it was helpful. If you'll excuse me, I have an estate to visit."

Danny brushed past the guild master and made his way out of the tower. If this guy was as rich as it sounded, finding him shouldn't be an issue. And once he did, Danny would be quick to learn the truth.

CHAPTER 28

D anny left the Wizards' Guild behind and turned toward the Adventurers' Guild. Thaddeus hadn't been as helpful as Danny had hoped, but he did provide some useful information. Grudgingly granted, but still useful. Finding Lord Carbey shouldn't be difficult, assuming he was as prominent as Thaddeus said. Given his reputation, Guild Master Lars should be able to point Danny in the right direction. Since Danny wanted to have a chat with the man anyway, this was the perfect chance to kill two birds with one stone.

A couple blocks from the Wizards' Guild, Danny activated his stealth field. At least for now, he didn't want word of his visit to Lars getting back to Berend. That would likely lead to a confrontation Danny preferred to avoid for the moment.

Noon was fast approaching, but the streets remained quiet. It would doubtless stay that way until the weather improved. Regardless, the lack of people made it easy for

Danny. Even the stealth field wouldn't keep someone from noticing if he bumped into them.

He reached the Adventurers' Guild and paused a few feet from the door. This was the tricky bit. He needed someone to open the door so he could slip in unnoticed.

Lucky for Danny, adventurers were frequently on the move regardless of the weather and after fifteen minutes the door finally swung open as a party of four heavily bundled people emerged. Danny darted past them a step ahead of the closing door.

The waiting room had a decent crowd. Most of the people were eating their lunch. The sight of so many tasty-looking dishes combined with the savory scent of roasted meat and fresh bread made Danny's mouth water. He shook his head. Business before food.

He wove his way toward the stairwell, slipping past tables and being careful not to bump into anyone. Silently he made his way to the third-floor landing where he found the closed door to Lars's office.

He gave it a couple soft knocks before stepping aside. A few seconds passed before the door opened and Lars stepped out, looking all around as he chewed his lower lip. Danny hadn't met the man yet and he wasn't terribly impressed. Adventurers tended to be hard, physically imposing people. Lars was many things, but none of them were imposing. He was a soft, slightly pudgy man dressed in pale silk. He reminded Danny a bit of the potion merchant Osbern. Not the most favorable comparison.

Danny slipped into the office and strode over to a huge wooden desk. There was nothing on it that resembled work, only a half-full glass of dark liquor sitting on a wooden coaster, some blank papers, and a quill and ink pot. The rest of the room was beautifully done in polished hardwoods, while gold and silver decorations glittered here and there and all the furniture was leather and well cushioned.

At a minimum this should be a physically comfortable conversation. Lars should share the name of his decorator with Thaddeus.

The door shut and Lars, frowning, took a step toward a still-invisible Danny. An effort of will conjured a sound barrier around the room. Best for everyone if this discussion stayed private. Precautions in place, Danny let the stealth field drop, revealing himself to the room's owner.

Lars's eyes widened and the blood drained from his face when he saw Danny. "Please, don't kill me. I haven't done anything to cross Berend, I swear." His words tumbled together in frantic haste. It was kind of pathetic for a guild master.

"Relax," Danny said. "I'm not here to hurt you. And I apologize for the abruptness of my appearance, but I thought it best if no one find out we had this chat."

The pounding pulse in Lars's neck slowed to something approaching normal. "You're not part of Berend's group?" he said like he didn't really believe it.

"I'm not part of anyone's group. My only interest is in finding a wizard named Avius who I'm pretty sure is responsible for the plague. The only reason I spoke to Berend was a man I trust said he was reliable. Since he's already lied to me once, I'm thinking I was misled."

Lars let out a shaky little laugh. "That's putting it mildly. What do you want from me?"

"Information. Let's start with Berend. What's his story?"

"He was part of a team of alpha elite adventurers. They were regarded as the best in Discourt. Everyone knew their names and they had a reputation for getting things done. And they did, but for every good thing they did for the city and the surrounding area, they did two things in secret that made things worse and them richer. Eventually rumors started to spread. Berend seized the moment and turned his own team in to the guards. He made himself look like a hero then helped his friends escape to continue their dirty work."

"Is that how he got his job with the guild?" Danny asked.

"Exactly right. He feeds his former associates intel and arranges jobs for them. Many of the younger adventurers look up to him and he uses that admiration to corrupt them and turn them into loyal followers. It's rather disgusting."

"Sounds like it. What are they up to now?"

Lars shook his head. "No idea. I used to try and keep tabs on Berend and his crew, but he made it clear that if I inter-fered no one would find my body. I'm no match for an alpha elite adventurer. Hell, I'm no match for a beginner. I do my best to keep my head down and listen. If I can warn any potential targets, I try to. But I'm unwilling to die for strangers."

Not terribly brave, but Danny admired his honesty if nothing else. So far, Lars hadn't said a single thing to set off his lie detection spell.

"Isn't there someone you could tell, someone in authority?"

"The lord mayor is nearly as corrupt as Berend. I wouldn't be surprised if they had some kind of deal going. Plus, any witnesses that might have spoken up are long dead. Best keep that in mind as you investigate."

Danny grinned. "I'm not so easy to kill. What about a guy named Lord Carbey? From what I've learned I think he might be harboring Avius. Do you know anything about him?"

Lars glanced toward the window then sighed. "Carbey? I don't think anyone knows anything about him. He showed up about fifteen years ago and bought up half the countryside. If that put any dent in his wealth it doesn't show. He's also got a mansion in the city, though according to his neighbors he's seldom there. Seems he prefers the country life."

"Where?" Danny asked.

"About twenty miles northwest of the city. I've never visited the place, but I doubt you'll have trouble finding it," Lars said. "The mansion is even harder to miss. It's built of imported marble and alabaster; the only one in the city, much to the lord mayor's chagrin."

"I appreciate your help." Danny held out his hand and Lars stared at it for a moment before shaking.

"Do you have any idea how long it's been since anyone shook my hand, much less spoke to me with respect?" Lars's voice cracked and Danny feared he might start crying. "You don't have to do this. Leave Discourt while you can and save yourself the trouble. You seem like a good man. I'd hate to see you end up like all the others."

"Your concern is much appreciated," Danny said. "But I mean to see this to the end. If Berend or Carbey or anyone else gets in my way, they'll wish they hadn't."

◯

Danny left the Adventurers' Guild and turned toward the merchants' district. In Villipan City it would've been called the noble district, but for some reason the people around here had problems with calling the rich and powerful nobles. Not that the name changed anything. People like Carbey were powerful regardless of what you called them.

He paused a block from the guild and bought a sandwich from a food stand. Much like on Earth, easily eaten foods at a good price were popular. Skewers, grilled sausages on sticks that reminded him of corn dogs without the pancake on the outside, and meat sandwiches of all sorts seemed to be the most popular.

Danny ate as he walked, his mind busy sorting the many bits of information he'd picked up. That Carbey and Avius were connected was undeniable at this point, but there was no evidence. Danny had no idea what he might find at the mansion, but figured a quick walk around the place might not be the worst idea.

If nothing else, showing his face might convince someone else to make a move. Of course the move was apt to be trying to kill Danny. Attempts on his life no longer bothered him the way they used to. He'd been nearly killed more times than he'd taken a proper bath on this world.

As for Berend, Danny wasn't sure what to think about the man. Everything Lars said about him rang true and Berend had already proven himself a liar. Prudence suggested it would be best to assume he was an enemy until he knew for sure otherwise.

He shook his head and popped the last bite of sandwich into his mouth. He was getting close, both to his destination and the truth. A little more digging, a bit of pushing, and he felt certain something would give. All around him the houses were getting nicer and nicer. It was time to focus on the matter at hand.

The merchants' district was an interesting place. It sat in

the center of the city and the deeper you went the nicer the places. Carbey's mansion was only a block from the lord mayor's residence and was by far the finer of the two buildings. It gleamed in the cold afternoon sun. Made of white stone and topped with a red tile roof, it was nearly as big as the temple of the Goddess. A garden planted with evergreen topiary surrounded it and a high fence made of black iron—the regular kind, not Hell forged—topped with ornate spikes, made it clear visitors were unwelcome.

Danny made a casual stroll around the perimeter. Guards patrolled the garden in groups of four. Their armor looked nearly identical to what the mercenaries at the elf outpost were wearing. He seriously doubted it was a coincidence.

Only one way to find out for sure.

Danny approached the front gate with calm but determined strides. Four guards armed with halberds were on duty. They eyed Danny the way he would a cockroach running across the dinner table.

"Good afternoon, gentlemen," he said. "I've got a message for Captain Koch from Assistant Guild Master Berend. It's about the beastfolk. I was hoping I could find him here."

One of the younger guards, a fresh-faced kid who'd probably never swung his sword in anger, said, "Captain Koch is out at the es—"

"Out of the city," an older guard said, silencing the younger man with a glare. "You can leave a message for him at the Mercenaries' Guild. He'll pick it up when he gets back."

"I should've thought of that, thanks." Danny meant it too. These two had kindly confirmed that Koch was working for Carbey which made one more link to Avius.

He left the guards and marched away from Carbey's

estate in the direction of the Mercenaries' Guild. He had no intention of visiting the place, but if anyone asked the guards where he went, they'd think he was actually a messenger completing his task.

Tonight, Danny would make another visit to the mansion. He'd seen no magical defenses and a fence guarded by some mercenaries wasn't nearly enough to keep him out. Whatever secrets were hiding in there, he'd find them.

CHAPTER 29

D anny stood, invisible, across the street from the wrought iron gate of Carbey's mansion. It was just after midnight and he had no doubt it was the coldest night of the year so far. The stars shone bright in the clear night sky. Every once in a while this world struck him with its beauty. Often at odd times, like right before breaking and entering.

Life was strange, no doubt.

Right, back to business. The gate guards had left for the night, but others still patrolled the garden. Flickering torch-light betrayed their movements. It might seem foolish to give away the position of your guards like that, but it made a certain amount of sense if the goal was to make it clear the place was under guard at night.

If they were trying to convince people not to break in, it wasn't working very well. Danny grinned, took a running start, sent ether into his legs, and leapt. He cleared the fence easily before landing silently on the manicured lawn. He paused, listening to the guards' steps crunching on the frozen grass. There was no sign he'd been noticed.

He sprinted to the front door and paused again. He sensed nothing directly beyond it. A quick jiggle confirmed the door was locked. A bit of ethereal manipulation popped the lock and he was inside.

The foyer was still and silent, the opulent furnishings draped in shadow. Danny opened himself to the ether. He sensed a few people on this floor, none upstairs, and at least twenty in the basement. Why the hell were there twenty people in the basement in the middle of the night? Or any other time of day for that matter.

Frowning, he made his way to a sweeping, grand staircase. Best to check the second floor first just to be sure. Danny took the steps two at a time. The second floor was every bit as well decorated as the first. There were paintings of all sorts, vases of fine porcelain, a couple suits of armor trimmed in gold, basically anything you could imagine someone with too much money in a fantasy world buying.

Danny methodically cleared each darkened room, confirming the absence of servants or guards. He found nothing save cloth-draped furniture. It was like no one lived here.

He found another staircase, this one way less fancy than the one he climbed, and started back down. Three-quarters of the way to the ground level, a faint scuffing caught Danny's attention. Sounded like someone was still up.

When he reached the floor, a flicker of movement from his left caught his eye. Danny hurried to catch up to whoever it was. A few strides later he heard voices.

"I never thought we were going to catch up to this one," a gruff male voice said.

"Right?" a different guy replied. "Hard to believe he took out team five. Must've gotten lucky."

He rounded a corner and found two black-armored soldiers carrying the limp form of a young man between them. He looked like the same kid Danny saved from being snatched off the streets just that morning. Talk about persistent, and did they really not know their boss or someone else blew the soldiers' heads to pulp?

Actually, they probably didn't. That wasn't the sort of thing you mentioned to your mercenaries.

Danny followed along behind them until the hall ended at a heavy oak door. The lead soldier held the kid's legs with one hand and yanked the door open with a grunt. Danny slipped through behind them. A stone staircase led down to the basement. The stink of waste and unwashed bodies did nothing to increase his optimism.

They stomped down the steps and at the bottom Danny stopped and stared. Whatever he'd been expecting, it wasn't this. Cages packed with exhausted, gaunt prisoners lined the walls. There were men, women, even a couple of kids younger than the new guy.

Opposite the cages, a figure in black robes hunched over a complex, bubbling alchemy setup. He was muttering something under his breath, but Danny couldn't make out what.

"Where would you like this one, sir?" the lead mercenary asked.

The wizard finally looked up. He had a handsome, lean face with a hawkish nose and hard, dark eyes. Danny assumed this was Avius. Or he hoped it was anyway. He'd dealt with all the flunkies he cared to.

"There's an empty cage in the back. Put him in there for now."

"No." Danny dropped his stealth field as he stepped forward. "You can just set him down, gently."

The soldiers looked from Danny to their employer as if uncertain what to do.

"You would be Ronin," the wizard said. "The adventurer who has been causing me so much trouble. I had hoped it would take you longer to find this place. Your arrival is inconvenient."

"Just to confirm, you're Avius, right?"

"Indeed. Now, if you'll run along, I need to return to my work. I'm so close to figuring out what went wrong."

"If you think I'm going to leave so you can create some new plague to let loose on the world, you're nuts. I'm ending you, right now."

"Idiot! I didn't create the plague, I only altered it to make divine healing less effective. Do you know what's wrong with the world?"

"Crazy wizards messing with diseases seems to be right up at the top of the list."

Avius shook his head, not reacting to Danny's taunt. "No. The problem is divine healing. Priests who think they're doing good are actually letting people who are meant to die, survive. It's making humanity weak. Each generation, flawed, defective people succeed in breeding, spreading their inferior lines and polluting the species."

"You really are nuts." Danny drew his sword.

As soon as he did, the soldiers dropped their burden and scrambled to put themselves between him and Avius.

"Do you know why beastfolk are stronger than humans?" Avius asked. "Because their shamans can't heal. For whatever reason, they have no true priests. The weak die and make the overall species stronger. Savage as they may be, at least their bloodlines are superior to humanity's. The plague was meant to remedy that by killing the weak and inferior."

"Weak and inferior!" Danny said. "I passed through a village a few weeks ago and your precious plague had killed everyone. I doubt they were all weaklings."

Avius sighed. "I'm sure they weren't. At some point, the plague mutated. It originally had a ninety percent survival rate. Now the survival rate has flipped and only ten percent live through it without magical intervention. I'm trying to determine what went wrong so I can stop it."

Danny's lie detection spell wasn't going off. Was this prick telling the truth? He couldn't decide if that was a good thing or a bad thing.

"Whatever you're trying to do, you can do it in public with the priests of the Goddess making sure you don't screw up again. If you really want to make things better, come along quietly."

"I can't do that." Avius threw out a hand and an invisible force picked Danny up and hurled him into the wall.

The impact drove the air out of his lungs and the soldiers were moving in fast.

Not bothering with his sword, Danny hurled lightning at both men, piercing their hearts and stopping them cold.

He glared at Avius. "Let's try that again."

"You're stronger than I expected." Avius's hands crackled with lightning of his own. "But not nearly strong enough."

Danny raised a shield an instant before a bolt of lightning came arcing in. The spells clashed, filling the air with blinding white light. At the rate they were going, some of the prisoners were going to end up caught in the crossfire.

Gritting his teeth, Danny pushed, sending Avius's own lightning into his face.

The wizard flew backwards, bounced off the floor, and rolled to his feet ten yards deeper into the basement.

"We'll finish this another day, boy." A flash of light brighter than the sun forced Danny to look away.

When his vision cleared, Avius was gone.

"Damn the man!" He sprinted down the hall past the cages. At the end of the passage he reached a blank wall where the sparkling, slowly fading remains of a spell circle told the tale. "A teleportation circle. Figures."

Avius could be anywhere now, though Danny had a strong suspicion that he fled to Carbey's country estate. According to Danny's inherited memories, you needed to prepare both ends of the teleportation spell, which meant he couldn't run just anywhere.

Well, he had no doubt he'd catch up to the wizard eventually.

Sheathing his sword, Danny hurried to the nearest cage and shattered the lock with a burst of magic. The terrified captives, three men and two women, flinched away from him. "It's alright, I'm not going to hurt you. Are you injured?"

The prisoners relaxed a fraction when it became clear he didn't intend them any harm. One of the men, a gray-bearded fellow about sixty, hesitantly asked, "Who might you be, sir?"

"Ronin. I'm an adventurer looking into the origin of the plague. I'd very much like to talk with you in more depth later, but for now, I need to free the other prisoners and get you all somewhere safe."

"Where might that be, sir?" the man asked. "These men grabbed us right off the street and no one did anything."

"My plan was to take you to the Goddess's temple. They've been helpful during my search and as far as I can tell, they're good people. You'll be safe there for now. Longer term, once I track down Avius and deal with him once and for all, the danger should be over. If you have an alternate idea, I'm happy to escort you wherever you'd like to go."

Danny backed out of the cage and moved on to the next one. It took about ten minutes but eventually he got everyone out. Though their clothes were in rough shape, they at least all had shoes. Thankfully the walk to the temple was a short one.

He led the group up into the mansion proper and out the front door into the freezing night. Fifteen mercenaries were arrayed in a semicircle in front of them. The soldiers all had their swords drawn.

"Go back inside where it's warm," Danny said. "I'll deal with them."

He didn't have to argue very hard to convince the former prisoners. Once the door had closed Danny focused on the mercenaries. "I'm going to make this real simple. Get lost and stay lost. Anyone still visible when I reach ten, is dead. One."

Danny counted slowly as the mercenaries looked at each other and at him. Part of him hoped they ran. But another part, the practical part, knew it would be easier to kill them now than to wait until they joined up with their buddies.

When he reached six one of the mercenaries said, "It's only one man. We can take him."

They roared and charged.

The soldiers managed three strides before an ethereal hand grenade exploded in their midst. The blast shook the mansion and sent bodies flying in every direction, none of them fully intact.

Danny shook his head at the pointlessness of it. No

matter their job, any sane person should see that setting these people free was the right thing to do.

The door eased open and one of the prisoners stuck his head out.

"It's over," Danny said. "Let's get you folks to the temple before the city guard shows up. I'd prefer to avoid any further violence tonight."

They all seemed enthusiastic about that plan and soon a ragged caravan was quick marching through the city. Some were carrying kids and two of the larger men lugged the still-unconscious youth between them.

By some mercy, they reached the temple without issue. Danny shoved the door open and ushered everyone in. The priestess on duty gaped as person after person staggered into the entry area.

When he'd shut the door Danny said, "I don't know who's in charge, but I've got a bunch of people in need of care. If you'd be so kind as to see to them, I'd be much obliged."

His words snapped her out of her stupor and she hurried into the infirmary to find help.

"We need to let our families know we're okay," someone said.

"I'm sure the temple will help you contact them," Danny said. "For now, let's focus on getting you checked out."

Soon the priestess returned with three of her fellows and they got busy sorting everyone out and guiding them into the infirmary. Danny yawned, happy to let them handle it. For now, all he wanted was a good night's sleep.

Tomorrow, he suspected, would be as busy if not busier than today.

CHAPTER 30

Danny sat with Mother Ankie in her bedroom, a delightful collection of goodies on the table between them. There were fried eggs, toast, sausage, sliced apples, and hot tea. As breakfasts went, this one was a winner. After a solid night's sleep, he'd come to update the high priestess and she'd suggested they talk over breakfast. Danny was quick to agree.

He swallowed a mouthful of tea and asked, "Does a mutating plague make any sense to you?"

Mother Ankie frowned. "I'm not familiar with the theory, but diseases do change over time, getting more or less severe. Why this should be I have no idea. The idea that anyone would be so foolish, or perhaps arrogant, to make a disease more resistant to magical healing is insane. Comparing us to beastfolk is also mad. We're different species for heaven's sake. Naturally there would be differences."

"Makes you wonder what made him think that way." Danny made a fist then forced himself to relax. "I can't believe I let the son of a bitch escape. Pardon my language."

Her frown turned into a smile. "I'm not the easily offended sort, despite what Father Koen might have you think. And don't beat yourself up. Freeing those people and driving Avius out of the city can only be a good thing."

Danny wished he was so confident. "What if he was right and his research is the only thing that can stop the new plague variant?"

"Even if he was," Mother Ankie said. "That doesn't give him the right to kidnap people, hold them in cages, and experiment on them. We'll have Thaddeus examine the lab. Perhaps he can come up with something."

A knock at the door cut their conversation short. Father Koen entered, his perpetual frown especially deep this morning. "Excuse the interruption, but there are guards outside, along with someone from the lord mayor's office. They're asking to speak with Ronin."

"They asked for me by name?" Danny asked.

"No, technically they asked for the person who blew up Lord Carbey's guards."

Danny grinned. That was close enough. He pushed back his chair and stood. "Guess I'd better see what they want."

Mother Ankie rose as well. "City officials tend to be more polite when a high priestess is around. I'll join you."

Danny's grin broadened and they set out together for the front door. As they walked Danny asked, "How were the prisoners?"

"We found no sign of illness," Mother Ankie said. "Other than being sleep deprived and hungry, they were fine. As far as the priests can tell, all Avius did was take a few blood samples from them. That supports his claim of searching for a cure rather than meaning them harm. Not that I would ever condone his actions."

In the foyer they found a group of six city guards clad in leather and chain mail shifting uneasily beside a man wrapped in a heavy, fur-trimmed cloak. He had a white, pointed goatee and the snooty, nose-in-the-air look of a man that hadn't done a real job in his entire life. This had to be the lord mayor's representative.

Danny disliked him at once.

"Mother Ankie," the official said, "I wasn't expecting you to join us."

"Ronin has been a great friend to the temple, not to mention saving my life. If you wish to cause him difficulty after all he's done for Discourt, it will be over my dead body."

The snooty fellow cleared his throat. "The mayor's office would never do anything to insult the Goddess's temple. But we do need to know exactly what happened last night. Your... friend woke up the entire neighborhood and when the guards arrived on the scene there were a number of bodies. Witnesses mentioned seeing a group of people fleeing the scene. Others saw them arrive here. It's hardly unreasonable that we have questions."

Danny might have underestimated this guy. He'd learned a great deal in eight hours.

"Of course, the temple understands the lord mayor has his duties as well. What time do you wish us to make our statement?"

"Would two hours be sufficient? His lordship has an opening in his schedule at that time."

"Your timeline is satisfactory," Mother Ankie said. "Tell the lord mayor we look forward to straightening out this situation."

The official bowed. "His lordship will no doubt be grateful for your willingness to help. Good morning."

When the official and his guards had left Mother Ankie said, "He won't rise far if he doesn't learn to lie better than that."

"What do you mean?" Danny hadn't renewed his lie detection spell yet this morning.

"I mean he didn't come here with six guards to ask you politely to stop by in a couple hours. They were going to grab you at sword point and drag you to the lord's manor right this second. No doubt they planned to make an example of you."

"I don't understand. I rescued a bunch of innocent people and drove off a crazy wizard. At minimum I should get a thank-you."

"You also broke into the home of one of the richest and most powerful landowners in Discourt. Not something Carbey's peers want to encourage. Heaven knows what sort of mischief they're getting up to. Not kidnapping and plague research hopefully, but that doesn't make them innocent either."

"Huh, I never really thought about it like that. I just did what needed doing."

Mother Ankie laughed. "And that's why you wouldn't make it far as a politician either. Don't worry, once it's clear you have the temple's support, the lord mayor will back off. His ego might be as big as the city, but he isn't stupid."

Danny hoped she was right. He had too much left to do and no intention of ending up in a cell or swinging from a rope. If the lord mayor wanted to push him, he'd find out Danny could push back.

D anny, Mother Ankie, and their temple knight
escort approached the lord mayor's residence, a
sprawling dark stone mansion that was built
more like a fortress. The place was only a block from
Carbey's mansion. Maybe the lord mayor was pissed because
Danny woke him up last night.

He wasn't quite sure what to expect with this meeting. As
far as Danny was concerned he'd done the right thing and
the twenty or so people he set free agreed.

"What's the lord mayor like?" Danny asked.

"Sajak is about what you'd expect. Greedy, venal, clever,
and arrogant. Sadly he was the best option we had during the
last election. I doubt next year will provide any better alter-
natives."

"Why not take the job yourself?" Danny asked.

Mother Ankie laughed. "I think not. I'm sure the city has
worse jobs, but none I less want to do. Besides, high priests
aren't eligible for the position. Neither are guild masters.
Only one of the landowners can be lord mayor. It's a way to
balance our power."

The group reached the heavy oak doors at the front of the
mansion. Like everything else about the place they had a
serious fortress vibe. On either side stood a pair of city
guards dressed in heavy cloaks. The nearest one on the right
slammed the butt of his halberd against the door.

When the door started to open the same guard said,
"You're expected. Go straight to the audience chamber. His
Lordship is waiting. Do you require a guide?"

"No," Mother Ankie said. "I've been here many times.
Thank you."

They strode through the open door. A few yards into the

entry hall Mother Ankie paused and turned to the knights. "You can wait for us here."

Danny thought they might argue, but the men just bowed and stepped to one side of the red carpet running deeper into the mansion.

"Seems a bit quiet," Danny said. "I expected more guards and servants."

"The servants are no doubt busy in the residence. There are guard stations at regular intervals, hidden behind special doors. If there's trouble, they can react in an instant but otherwise they stay out of sight. It makes the public area feel more welcoming. In theory at least."

Danny concentrated and immediately sensed the hidden guards, about twenty of them in two groups of ten. That still seemed like too few, but whatever. He wasn't in charge of security. And if someone did something stupid, like try and arrest him, at least Danny knew how many soldiers he'd have to defeat.

The carpet ended at an archway beyond which was a large, open room. At the far end of the space a single figure sat on an ornate throne. The man himself was wrapped in a purple, fur-trimmed robe that tried to swallow him up. The only thing missing was a crown.

"The lord mayor, I take it?" Danny asked.

"Indeed," Mother Ankie said. "Sajak likes to play at being a king though he only has what authority the city council grants him. Try to humor him unless he gets too obnoxious."

Mother Ankie stopped a few strides from the throne. "Mayor Sajak. We've come as requested. Allow me to introduce Ronin, the heroic adventurer who risked his own life to rescue a number of our kidnapped citizens."

Danny bowed. "Pleasure to meet you, sir."

Sajak's gaunt face twisted into something ugly. "Mother Ankie. So kind of you to come all this way after your recent illness. It was hardly necessary."

"On the contrary," she said. "Ronin is a great friend of the temple. We owe him a debt, not least for saving my life."

"I see. The temple of the Goddess plans to defend this criminal. How disappointing."

The accusation rankled, but Danny had to admit he did break the law. That he'd done it to save people didn't change the facts.

"Is it the intention of the mayor's office to arrest and put on trial a man who rescued innocent people from the most deplorable conditions? No doubt the people will be thrilled to see how you're keeping them safe."

Sajak's frown deepened. "If Mr. Ronin had evidence that people were being held in Carbey's mansion, he should've brought it to the city guards. Investigating crimes is their job, not some random adventurer's."

Danny took a deep breath. "I didn't have any evidence to offer until I infiltrated Carbey's mansion. Once I found those people locked up and the wizard responsible for the plague experimenting on them, I couldn't walk away and leave them alone."

Sajak's brows furrowed as he listened. "Breaking into a citizen's home, no matter the reason, is a crime. How would it look if the law looked away because the outcome of the crime ended up being good?"

"It would look like the law recognized a good deed when it saw one," Mother Ankie said. "You know people already think the wealthy and powerful can get away with murder. If you punish the man that stood up to one of them when they tried, you might have a riot on your hands. We'll be reuniting those freed with their families today and telling them exactly how they got their loved ones back."

Sajak steepled his fingers, eyes narrow. "That sounded like a threat."

"Not at all, Sajak." Mother Ankie continued as if he hadn't spoken. "In fact, Carbey's actions have shown a blatant disregard for the safety and well-being of Discourt. Surely, such behavior cannot go unpunished. Confiscating his estate would send a clear message to other landowners that harboring enemies of the city will not be tolerated."

Sajak's narrow eyes widened. "There may be something to your argument. Very well, I'm willing to overlook Ronin's illegal actions since they were for the good of the city. However, I must warn you, Ronin, that taking matters into your own hands a second time will not be tolerated."

Danny nodded. "I understand, sir."

"Good. You're dismissed. Mother Ankie, I'll see you at the next council meeting."

"Indeed, I'll be sure to let the other high priests know how dedicated you are to the greater good. Until then."

Danny bowed and Mother Ankie offered a polite nod before they turned to leave the audience chamber. As they retraced their steps back to the exit, Danny considered what Sajak's words meant for his investigation. Since Avius had, he assumed, left the city, it didn't make much difference what the lord mayor said.

They picked up their escort and headed for the temple. As they walked Danny asked, "Is it going to be a problem if I investigate Carbey's country estate?"

"Not at all. Sajak's authority doesn't extend beyond the city walls. But understand, that means the estate will be much more heavily guarded than the mansion. Take care not to get in over your head."

Danny grinned. If she'd had any idea some of the things he'd done in Villipan, she wouldn't be worried about him visiting some rich guy's estate. "I appreciate the warning, ma'am. Rest assured, I'll be careful."

○

Avius looked from Berend to Koch and back. The trio was seated at the dining room table at Carbey's country estate. When he selected these two as his partners in the project, he'd had high hopes. The plan had been going reasonably well until the plague mutated. That turn of events had been wholly unexpected. His goal of strengthening humanity may well end up largely erasing it, at least in this area.

A disappointing result to be sure, but the disease didn't linger long enough to spread across the world. Humanity would survive, albeit in its degraded form.

The immediate problem was the adventurer Ronin. The man was proving a bigger problem than Avius had dreamed possible. Far from recovering the current project, Avius was more worried about surviving.

He leaned forward, steepling his fingers. None of his worries showed through his calm exterior. Only their fear of his wrath kept his partners in line. Should they lose that, he would have a rebellion to deal with in addition to his other problems.

"Ronin will be coming," he said. "It's only a matter of when. We need to be ready to deal with him."

Captain Koch slammed a fist on the table. "Damn it,

Avius! I've lost too many men on this job. At the rate we're burning through them I may lose my seat at the Mercenaries' Guild too. I want a bonus."

Berend chuckled. "Perhaps if your men were more competent, Captain, they'd still be alive."

"My men are the finest fighters in the region. We had no trouble rounding up all those beastfolk your friends took north."

"And you got your cut from the sale," Berend said. "Spare me your whining now that we've run into a real obstacle."

Berend was vastly understating the precariousness of the situation, but Avius agreed with his attitude. Had he known ahead of time what a simpering fool Koch was, he would've hired a different captain.

"You will be compensated," Avius said. "The merchants will be back with the proceeds from the first batch of cure potions in the spring. That will provide plenty of wealth to go around. Pity we'll need to reclaim the outpost before another batch can be prepared, but the circumstances are what they are. For the moment let's focus on dealing with Ronin."

"I'll handle him," Berend said. "But I'll need more men to make my plan work."

"I have six elite swordsmen left," Koch said. "They're my best fighters. Take them and end this."

"Six will suffice. They should be plenty to handle one man. We'll ambush him on the road leading to the estate. I know the perfect spot. We'll surround him and attack all at once."

Avius considered the plan. A simple ambush seemed unlikely to succeed, but then again, sometimes simple was best. "Be careful, Ronin's magic impressed me. There aren't many people strong enough to force me to flee, even weary as I was. Underestimate him and you'll pay the price."

Berend snorted and waved away Avius's warning. "Magic doesn't frighten me, not when I'm wearing the mask and cloak. And no one can best me with a blade. Besides, Ronin trusts me. I'll get close and cut him down. Even if he survives the first blow, six men are more than adequate to deal with a weakened enemy."

"So be it," Avius said. "I leave this matter in your hands, Berend. Bring me good news. In the meantime, I'll be in my lab. Freeing the survivors may have set me back, but I have sufficient blood samples to keep going."

Avius stood and stalked out of the dining room. Maybe it was wishful thinking to imagine he could still turn this debacle around, but he'd invested too much of his life to give up now.

CHAPTER 31

The wind howled, biting through Danny's cloak as he trudged along the snow-covered road. Flurries stung his eyes, forcing him to squint. The weather had gone from cold to frozen hellscape in the six hours since he left Discourt. The sky was so dark he could barely see the dirt road under his feet. All in all it was a perfect day for hunting down an insane wizard.

He had no idea how far he'd come or how far he had left to go. The directions he'd gotten to Carbey's estate didn't include precise distances, only that if he kept a steady pace he should arrive before sunset. Father Koen had said before dark, but it was plenty dark already.

A frown creased his face when he sensed a life force directly ahead. Danny looked up from his boots. A dark figure stood in the middle of the road about fifty yards ahead. He couldn't make out any details beyond the silhouette and the snapping ends of a black cloak. Who the hell would be out in this weather?

Danny moved his hand to the hilt of his sword and

expanded his awareness. As he feared, he sensed six more people just over the crest of a nearby hill. They were at the very edge of his range and would likely be undetectable to anyone else. Someone, it seemed, was setting a trap.

They were also directly in his path. Seeing no way to avoid the fight, Danny trudged onward.

Ten yards out a familiar voice said, "Ronin, I was afraid I wouldn't find you in time."

"Berend? What are you doing out here? And why are you looking for me?"

Berend moved a little closer. Danny shifted back, maintaining the gap. Given the hidden men and what he knew about the assistant guild master, Danny had no intention of letting him close to easy sword range.

"Are you planning to force me to shout my message?" Berend asked, his tone incredulous.

"I had a long conversation with Lars," Danny said. "That, along with the six people you've got hiding just out of sight make me hesitant to let you come too close."

The storm hid Berend's expression, but Danny doubted it was pleased. "It's unfortunate that you've been taken in by his lies. As for the people you mentioned, I know nothing about them. I came alone."

Every word a lie. Disappointing, but hardly a surprise.

"Take your friends and go," Danny said. "I have other business today."

Berend reached under his cloak and pulled out a black mask carved in the likeness of a demon. "This would've been less painful for you if you'd let me make your end quick. Now we have to do it the hard way."

He put the mask in place and drew a slim, slightly curved sword.

Danny's sword cleared its sheath an instant later.

Ether crackled around his free hand and he hurled a bolt of lightning at Berend.

The blast hit his black cloak and fizzled, a few sparks floating out into the darkness.

Berend charged, his movements sharp and skilled.

But so slow it was a joke.

Danny turned the first blow aside and charged his body with ether. A hard slash sent Berend flying ten yards back. His cloak might turn aside spells, but it did nothing to lessen the power of Danny's physical enhancement. And that was all he needed to deal with an ordinary man, no matter how skilled.

Berend skidded to a halt, loosed a piercing whistle, then came charging back in.

He had guts, Danny had to give him credit for that. A moment later he sensed the hidden force come charging their way. Pointless, unless they were all immune to magic.

Danny punched Berend in the face, sending him sprawling in the dirt. One problem taken care of, he turned to the six new ones charging down the nearby hill. Black-armored mercenaries like the ones who kidnapped that kid in Discourt were headed his way, swords drawn.

Another, more powerful bolt of lightning lanced out, arcing from soldier to soldier and burning them out. In less than a second all six were lying still in the snow.

Against anyone else, it would've been a good ambush, but Danny wasn't just anyone else. After fighting demons and giants, men, no matter how talented, didn't compare.

"Who are you?" Berend stared up at him through the holes in his mask. "No first-year adventurer has that kind of power."

Danny flicked the man's mask off with the tip of his sword. Blood leaked down Berend's lip from where Danny hit him.

"I'm no one special, just an adventurer trying his best to make the world a better place. Was that ever your goal or were you always a corrupt piece of shit?"

Berend's laugh was bitter. "The world doesn't want to be saved, boy. It's full of ugly, grubby, self-serving assholes who are all out to get what they can and if you stand in their way, they'll step on you without a second thought. The only way to win, to survive, is to be the strongest and nastiest. I did what I had to and make no apologies."

"Your apologies wouldn't interest me anyway. Tell me about Avius and whatever defenses I'll have to deal with at the estate."

Berend remained silent.

"Don't mistake my desire to do good as an unwillingness to do hard things." Danny flicked his wrist, opening a deep gouge across Berend's cheek. "Talk, or next time I'll cut one of your eyes out."

A pained grimace twisted Berend's face. "It seems I underestimated you in more than one way. Three squads of infantry and one squad of archers are on duty defending the estate. Koch is there as well, not that the miserable pissant is worth a damn in a fight. Avius is neck deep in research. It seems he doesn't want to wipe out ninety percent of the world's population."

"Yet he had no issue with killing ten percent."

Berend shrugged. "He pays well and made me immune. I wasn't terribly concerned if a bunch of weak, sickly wastes of space ended up dead. Even getting rid of ninety percent might not be such a bad thing. The world would be a better place without ninety percent of the people I've met."

"You've clearly been hanging around with the wrong people. Enjoy an eternity in whatever hell is waiting to claim you."

Berend smiled, showing no sign of fear. "I'll be waiting for you."

A quick slash removed his head from his neck.

Danny sighed, cleaned the blood off his sword, and sheathed it. It was a shame Berend was such a lunatic. With his skill, he could've helped a lot of people. But that was the way it went sometimes.

Danny collected his mask and cloak, folded them into a neat bundle, and hid them under a tree near the edge of the road. No way was he putting something resistant to magic in his storage. For all he knew it might collapse the whole thing. No, he'd collect both items on his way back.

Next he took Berend's sword and gave it a few swings. The balance and heft were exquisite, far nicer than the bandit's sword Danny was still using. It was plain if high quality steel and he could detect no magical properties. Should be safe to upgrade.

He put his own sword and baldric in storage and belted on Berend's. Business concluded, Danny started walking. The fight had warmed him up a bit, but the cold was already seeping back in. It couldn't be far to the estate and he wanted to get there before he froze or someone else tried to kill him.

CHAPTER 32

D anny had thought Carbey's mansion in Discourt was huge, but his country estate put the mansion to shame. The main house was easily half again as big. There were six outbuildings scattered around, each of them bigger than most people's homes. The whole compound was surrounded by a twenty-foot-tall steel fence with a single entrance guarded by ten soldiers. Drifting magical lights illuminated the area, revealing the rest of the patrolling soldiers. It was an impressive setup, no doubt.

At least, it would've been to anyone besides Danny. He went to the west side of the fence where no patrols were visible, took the ethersword out of storage, and sliced an opening out of the bars. He could've used his stealth field and snuck in, but saw no particular point. He was going to end up fighting everyone inside anyway, so he might as well get on with it.

He strode across the frozen grass, lit sword in hand, and waited for one of the patrols to spot him. That took less than a minute.

"Halt!" a soldier shouted. "You're trespassing on private property. Surrender at once."

At this point the three patrolling squads had converged and surrounded Danny. That was handy.

He channeled ether through the mithril hilt then blasted it outward in every direction. A wave of power picked the men up and hurled them across the yard, scattering them like bowling pins.

When the spell faded, he was pleased to see all of them had survived albeit with lots of broken bones. These soldiers at least wouldn't be troubling him anytime soon. He continued on to the main house. It had a pair of massive oak doors that would've looked more at home on a castle than a gentleman's mansion.

Danny checked them for wards and found a basic locking spell as well as an alarm set to alert the caster. Unless Avius was unconscious or dead, there was no way he hadn't sensed Danny's earlier spell. That made the alarm irrelevant.

Three slashes turned the no-doubt-expensive door into firewood.

Danny marched through the opening and focused. Only one life force in the place. He had a pretty good idea who that was. Avius was on the first floor rather than in the basement.

Weird, but then again, everything about this place was weird. Especially the lack of people. What was the point of having all this space if you were going to keep it empty?

Whatever, none of it mattered. Homing in on Avius's position, Danny strode through empty rooms untroubled by guards or magic. A dozen yards away, the ether began to stir. Avius was doing something magical, though Danny wasn't nearly skilled enough to say exactly what.

He strode through another door and something slammed into his back, staggering him a step. Snarling, he spun and found a weaselly looking little man holding a dagger with a bent blade. Giving a silent word of thanks to his personal shield, Danny closed in on the man.

"Please don't kill me, please don't kill me, please don't kill me." Tears and snot ran down his face as he waved the bent dagger in front of Danny.

"You must be Koch," Danny said. "For a mercenary captain, you're not terribly impressive."

Koch let out a hysterical giggle. "You're not the first to say so, but there's more to being a good captain than fighting ability. My specialty is organization, very important you know."

As a former Marine, Danny knew that very well. "Is there any reason I shouldn't just cut your head off and move on to your employer?"

"I wish you wouldn't say that so casually." Koch wiped the sleeve of his no-doubt-expensive tunic across his face. At least the threat of imminent death had focused him a bit. "Spare me and I'll do whatever you want. It's going to take me years to rebuild after this debacle. I know everything. I can tell you everything, at least everything not directly relating to the magic. That I don't understand at all."

"I like your attitude. You'll wait here while I deal with Avius."

"Of course I—" Danny's left fist hit him like a sledgehammer, dropping Koch to the floor.

He toed him over on his back. His breathing was steady and it looked like no major damage was done. Good, the powers that be would no doubt be eager to hear what this clown had to say.

Now, for the head man himself. Danny worked his way deeper into the house, homing in on the final life force. There were no further attacks and eventually he reached an open door with bright light pouring out. Beyond was an alchemy lab and Avius, standing in front of a large table covered with bubbling flasks and dripping alembics. Talk about déjà vu.

The wizard turned slowly towards him, his face a weary mask of resignation. Not exactly the expression you expected to see on someone about to fight to the death.

"Will nothing I say convince you to let me finish my work? It may be the world's only hope."

Danny lowered the ethersword a fraction but didn't deactivate it. "I doubt you really care about the world. If you did, you never would've changed the plague in the first place."

Avius shook his head. "Something had to change. Humanity was growing weaker all the time. This world is dangerous. There are threats everywhere, monsters, demons, other men, plague, famine, you name it. The weakest members of our species could drag us all down and Heaven does its best to help them do it. The priests claim the archangels love us. If that's true, why do they want us weak?"

"That's some seriously screwed-up reasoning. Being physically weak doesn't make you useless. There are many brilliant people with bodies you would consider flawed. Their contributions to society can't be overlooked. What if your plague kills the next genius wizard who will advance magical knowledge a hundred years?"

"You can't know that," Avius said.

"Neither can you! Neither can the archangels. Don't you think that has more to do with why they want to save everyone they can?"

Avius stared at him, eyes wide and chin trembling. "I never thought about it that way. The plague nearly killed me when I was a child. There was no priest in our little community to save me. When I recovered, my parents said I was strong, a worthy member of the group. It was only later, when I traveled, that I learned about healing magic and how others didn't have to suffer as I did. The more I saw the pathetic state of the people who led humanity, the more I thought things had to change. If suffering brings strength, I would make humanity suffer."

"Thus the super plague. And now it's run out of control."

"Yes. Despite my best efforts, I can find no way to change it back." Avius blew out a long sigh. "I wanted to make humanity better, stronger. Instead I've doomed it. You may as well kill me now. I deserve nothing less."

"There is another option," Danny said. "If you're serious about improving humanity."

Avius frowned. "What do you mean?"

"You made your followers immune to the plague. Why can't you repeat the process on everyone else? Instead of increasing suffering, you could eliminate at least some of it."

"That... is a possibility I hadn't considered. The process isn't especially difficult, but I couldn't do it on my own to everyone."

"I wouldn't trust you to, but I'll wager the temple of the Goddess would make a good partner for you. You teach them how to do it and they'll spread the knowledge to the far corners of the world. They're already planning a healing caravan to cure the local victims. They could also render everyone they meet immune at the same time. In a generation, the plague would be nothing but a memory. This plague at least. This is your chance to really help humanity, if you're willing to take it."

Avius drew himself up straight. "I accept your terms. I've been a fool; I see that now. I swear, I'll spend the rest of my life trying to make amends. I never should've listened to Berend."

Danny frowned. "What did he say? I thought you were the leader of this project?"

"I am, but he put the kernel of the idea in my mind. We first met in an elf ruin. I was seeking knowledge and he and his team wealth and magic. We got to talking and it seemed I'd found a kindred spirit. Berend was as disillusioned with humanity, especially its leaders, as I was. He said they were a plague on the world. That was when it all clicked."

"Then it's a good thing I killed him. We'll spend the night here and set out in the morning. I have no interest in venturing out into that storm."

"Whatever you decide. I'll gather and organize my notes."

Avius started to turn but one other thing was nagging at Danny. "Where's Carbey in all this? Despite all I've heard about the guy, I've yet to see any sign of him."

"You've already met him," Avius said. "I'm Carbey. I created him as an alter ego, a front I could use to spend the considerable wealth I gained from exploring elf ruins. One of the artifacts I found generates an illusion that also suppresses my magical aura. When I'm posing as Carbey, you'd never know I was a wizard. On the downside, I can't use magic while I'm wearing the amulet."

"That makes things easier. When we leave in the morning, you'll do so as Carbey. I assume there's a carriage and some horses somewhere on this estate. It'll save a lot of trouble when we reach Discourt. That reminds me." Danny stepped closer and touched Avius's arm. A surge of ether burned a mark into it, drawing a flinch and pained hiss from the wizard. "There, now I can find you wherever you might run to."

"I have no intention of running," Avius said.

"Good. I have no desire to hunt you down again. See you in the morning."

Danny left Avius to his work. He needed to drag the soldiers inside before they froze to death then find somewhere to rest. While he knew the plague wasn't completely dealt with, at least now it felt like they had a path to victory. He couldn't say exactly what he'd expected when he finally ran the wizard down, but a depressed old man with twisted if vaguely positive intentions hadn't made the list.

Hopefully Mother Ankie and the other priests would be able to make use of his knowledge to quickly spread immunity across the world.

At a minimum, Danny felt confident he could move on to Elfhome. There was also the matter of the missing beastfolk slaves. He'd like to find and rescue them, but if they'd been sold and scattered to the winds, it would be no easy task. Traveling in this miserable weather wouldn't be pleasant either, but he was determined not to delay any further.

CHAPTER 33

T he next morning saw Danny on the road again, this time riding in a fancy carriage and surrounded by a small force of mercenaries who hadn't been so badly injured they couldn't move. Avius and Koch were seated across from him, the latter rubbing his jaw now and then. The most remarkable thing, aside from the soft cushions, was Avius's transformation into Carbey. He'd put the amulet on before they left the mansion and the illusion settled over him like a second skin. Danny had never seen anything like it. There was no sign in the ether that the man was a wizard.

On a related note, all of Avius's magical gear and research was safely locked up in Danny's storage. Though he'd shown no sign of trying to escape, Danny felt better now that he had the information they needed secured.

"What will we do when we reach Discourt?" Koch asked.

"We'll go straight to the temple," Danny said. "Mother Ankie knows the ins and outs of city politics and I'm content to let her figure out the right move. As far as I'm concerned, once I drop you two off, my job is done. I plan to be on my way to Elfhome tomorrow."

Avius cocked his head. "I wouldn't recommend it."

"Why?"

"I tried to visit the city years ago and found it guarded by a demon, a very powerful demon. I barely escaped with my life."

"What sort of demon was it?" Danny had fought plenty of demons and his idea of a really strong one and Avius's might be different.

"I don't know her technical name. She looked nearly human, dressed all in black, and had wings like a raven. I've fought and defeated minor demons before, but this creature was on an entirely different level."

"I appreciate the warning, but I still have to go. Some information I need can only be found there." Danny wasn't sure that was true, but Elfhome was the only place he could think of to find what he sought.

Avius shrugged. "It's your life, spend it as you wish."

The conversation ebbed after that and an hour later Danny spotted the tree where he left Berend's cloak and mask. What he didn't see was seven bodies by the side of the road. He saw six. That couldn't be good.

"Tell the driver to stop. I need to check something."

Avius pulled the curtain aside and poked his head out. "Pull over, driver."

They clattered to a stop and Danny jumped out. He trotted over to the bodies and as he feared there was no sign of Berend's. Even in this world he doubted a headless corpse got up and walked away on its own. Even worse, the ether had a corrupt feel. It was faint but definitely present. He didn't know what happened here, but whatever it was, it couldn't be good.

He went over to the tree and blew out a sigh of relief. The mask and cloak were waiting where he left them. Danny grabbed them and turned to find Avius standing near the bodies. He'd removed his amulet and was studying the area intently.

"See anything interesting?" Danny asked.

"A hell portal opened here."

Shit! That was so not what Danny was hoping to hear. "You're sure?"

"As sure as I can be given how much the ether has already repaired itself. It seems Berend made plans for his future. I wonder which demon lord he offered his soul to."

Danny had a bad feeling he was going to find out far sooner than he wanted to. He focused on the remaining bodies and reduced them to nothing with a disintegration spell.

"Hey!" Koch shouted from the carriage. "That black armor isn't cheap."

Danny had no sympathy for either the dead men or their leader. "Let's get out of here."

Avius restored the amulet and they returned to the carriage. Danny set the cloak and mask on the seat beside him. It was a relief to set it down. Just holding the black cloth made him feel weird.

"Where did you find those?" Avius nodded toward the cloak.

"Berend. They disrupted attack spells targeted at him. Bloody nuisance, but luckily for me they didn't affect my physical enhancements."

"May I see it?" Avius asked.

Danny couldn't see any harm and passed the cloak over. Avius held it up to the light passing through the curtain. The cloth sparkled like something a Vegas magician might wear when making a casino disappear.

"Amazing." Avius barely breathed the word. "This cloak is woven with threads of anti-mithril. It repels the ether, rendering anyone wearing it or wielding a weapon made of it invincible to direct attack spells. You can't begin to imagine how rare that metal is."

"I'd like to throw it in my storage and forget about it forever, but I'm afraid it'll disrupt the magic."

"Very wise. You need to place it inside something first, like a chest. That will contain the effect and you'll be able to safely lock it away."

Danny took the cloak back. "How do you know all this?"

"I read about it in the journal of an elf-blood wizard obsessed with the stuff. Berend likely found the cloak in one of his labs."

Great, metal that repelled magic, one more thing he'd have to worry about. If it was as rare as Avius made out, at least it shouldn't be a common problem. No one felt much like chatting after that and the rest of the journey passed in silence. Dusk was approaching when the walls of Discourt appeared ahead of them.

The carriage slowed and a gruff voice asked, "Name and purpose of your visit to Discourt?"

"Lord Carbey's carriage returning from his country estate," the driver said. "It's quite chilly and his lordship is eager to get home."

Danny grinned. If being a mercenary didn't work out, the driver had a future as an actor.

"Go on in," the guard said.

A moment later they were moving. The driver knew where to take them and a ten-minute ride ended outside the Goddess's temple. Danny got down and stretched. For all that he complained about walking everywhere, he'd gotten used to it. The long ride left him stiff.

"What should I do?" Koch asked.

"You'll stay with us," Danny said. "Your guys are free to return to their barracks or wherever they stay between jobs. They can take the carriage with them. Once we talk with Mother Ankie, we'll see what's next."

Koch gave the order and soon it was just the three of them. Danny led the way up to the temple and pushed through the front door. The warmth felt wonderful. Michael's girlfriend was on duty behind the welcome desk.

She offered a hesitant smile, her gaze darting between Danny, Avius, and Koch. "Is everything okay?"

"I'm not sure yet. Is Mother Ankie available? We have some important matters to discuss with her. Father Koen should probably attend as well."

"I'll check, please wait here." She left the table and hurried deeper into the temple.

"Do you think she'll see us?" Avius asked.

"I expect so. She's been waiting for me to return with news."

Sure enough, ten minutes later they were guided to a meeting room three doors down from Mother Ankie's bedroom. She and Father Koen were seated at a rectangular table. They stood when Danny and his…prisoners? That didn't seem quite right. Whatever, it didn't matter what he called them.

"Welcome back, Ronin," Mother Ankie said. "Please sit and tell us what you've learned."

Danny obliged and when he finished, the normally good-natured high priestess was glaring with full fury at Avius. "That might be the most evil thing I've ever heard of. You, sir, belong in the deepest, darkest hell imaginable."

"I did what I thought best for humanity. That it turned out poorly is unfortunate." Avius spoke with a stone-cold poker face. If Mother Ankie's wrath troubled him in the least, he gave no sign. "For now we need to focus on setting things right. Ronin's suggestion is ambitious, but if the temple is willing to work with me, it should be possible."

Mother Ankie turned to Danny. "Do you trust him?"

"Not especially, but I do think he wants to keep the bulk of humanity from dying. As long as you keep an eye on him, it should be okay. I've got all his research, so you can confirm what he says. And as long as he keeps the amulet on, he can't use magic. I think the gains are worth the risks. As for Koch, I thought he could speak to the lord mayor and explain that Berend was really responsible for everything and that Avius died in the battle. Lord Carbey is deeply saddened that he was so badly deceived by his retainer and would like to donate his country estate to make amends. I suspect that will end any official concerns."

Mother Ankie's stern expression cracked into a faint smile. "You're a quick learner. Very well. The temple will work with Avius to spread plague immunity across the world. Father Koen, you will be in charge of Avius and the overall project. I will reach out to the other high priests to let them know what's happening. The more prepared they are, the faster they'll be able to deploy the magic once we have it perfected. You two should get started."

Father Koen took the hint and stood. "Follow me. We have a proper magical workshop in the rear of the temple."

"One moment." Danny opened his storage and pulled out all the research materials he'd collected. "You'll need these."

Father Koen grunted as he hefted the stack of books and papers. All three men stepped out of the room leaving Danny and Mother Ankie alone.

"What will you do now?" she asked.

"I feel like this matter is reasonably under control," Danny said. "I'm not good at research or precise casting. If I tried to help I'd just be in the way. No, I think it's time I got back to my own mission. I'll be leaving tomorrow to continue my journey. Miserable as the weather is, I still should be able to make some progress."

"I'm most grateful you were here in our hour of need and not only because you saved my life. Heaven knows what might've happened if you hadn't intervened. Whatever your plans going forward, I wish you only the best. May the Goddess go with you."

Danny smiled. "She certainly may. Would it be possible to impose on you to have the caravan deliver a couple letters for me?"

"Certainly. In fact, I wish I could offer you some other sort of reward, but I fear the temple will need all its resources to deal with the current emergency."

"Don't worry about it," Danny said. "I helped out because it was the right thing to do, not because I expected to get rich. It's been a pleasure, Mother Ankie. If I'm ever back this way, I'll be sure to stop by. Good luck with the cure."

He stood, offered a polite bow, and strode out. He needed supplies, then he'd find a new inn and write his letters. First thing in the morning he'd drop them off and it would be time to hit the road.

Elfhome was waiting.

BONUS CHAPTER – THE FIVE KINGDOMS RECOVERY PLAN PART 1

L yra strode through the halls of Castle Villipan. Things were largely back to normal now. Servants scurried around, their minds free of demonic influence. A hint of chill filled the air despite the best efforts of the castle's many fireplaces. Six inches of snow covered the ground outside, making travel miserable. Everyone was hunkered down as they waited for spring.

Once the weather turned nice, she was less confident about the future. Alban Morel had basically moved into the castle and he spent all his time whispering in King Florian's ear. The wretch had ambitions and he was trying to spread them. So far, Florian had shown little sign of wanting to play along, but Lyra figured it was only a matter of time.

She reached the war room and pushed the door open. Eve was there, but the rest of the group had yet to join the youthful priestess. Her already pale skin looked bone white today and dark circles surrounded her eyes. Clearly Eve hadn't been sleeping well.

She smiled at Lyra and started to stand. Lyra waved her back and settled in the chair beside her.

"Lady Shael, you're looking well."

"You're not," Lyra countered with typical bluntness. "What's troubling you?"

"I've been thinking about Daniel, wondering where he was and what he's doing. I wish he'd decided to stay." Eve hesitated then added, "I don't like the way things are going. Duke Alban asked me the other day whether Adonael would allow us to fight with the army if it wasn't against the demon king. I told him if Villipan was attacked, we'd do our best to help, but Adonael would condemn a war of aggression. I'm uncertain what he's planning, but I hope I dissuaded him."

Lyra had heard nothing about another war and liked the sound of it not in the least. Who would they fight? The Five Kingdoms was in rough shape after the demon king's invasion. Villipan's army was barely worthy of the name, with less than fifteen percent of the soldiers still in any condition to fight.

Before Lyra could ask for more details, the door opened again and Florian, Alban, and General Gaul entered together. The king and duke were both smiling and seemed in high spirits. The general, on the other hand, looked like a starving ghoul had eaten his cat.

"You're all here, excellent," Florian said. "After much consultation with Lord Morel, I've come to some decisions about Villipan's future."

Lyra's stomach twisted. Florian looked far too pleased with himself.

"After this most recent debacle," Florian said. "It has become clear to us that in order to survive, it has become necessary to reunite the Five Kingdoms in a single kingdom, the Kingdom of Greater Villipan."

He paused, looking from Lyra to Eve and back as though he expected them to burst into applause. Reuniting the kingdoms was among the stupidest ideas Lyra had heard in some time. If he'd suggested absorbing Forte, she could've seen it. The royal family was dead and most of the population scattered or sacrificed. Someone was going to have to step in and restore order for the survivors. But the rest of the kingdoms were another matter. No one had even visited them to see how things stood.

When the silence had stretched to an uncomfortable length Lyra asked, "How did you plan to go about it?"

Florian beamed at her. "Alban came up with a brilliant idea. We're going to summon another hero to lead our army. With his power at our disposal, the other kingdoms will be quick to surrender and become vassal states."

All eyes turned to Eve, who quickly waved her hands. "That's not at all possible. It takes a full century for the cathedral's magic to recover. Besides, the hero summoning is only for fighting the demon king."

"Are you refusing to carry out your king's command?" Alban asked.

"It's not a question of obeying or not." Eve drew herself to her full if rather unintimidating height. "I'm only a conduit for Adonael's power. If His Majesty can command an archangel to grant me the power, I will be happy to obey. Should Adonael decide not to comply with the king's command, there's nothing I can do."

Lyra refrained from smiling, much as she wanted to. The idea of Florian commanding an archangel was hilarious.

That Villipan was stuck with the fool as king was less hilarious.

"Is it truly impossible, Eve?" Florian asked.

"Yes, Majesty, it is," Eve said with a firmer tone than Lyra had ever heard her use. "The summoning ritual was created to counter the demon lord's champion, not to increase Villipan's territory or fight allies we'll need when the current and still very much alive demon king returns. Rather than fighting amongst ourselves, we should be rebuilding the combined army and preparing for the next round of the current war."

Alban snorted. "We do not need military advice from a woman. If you cannot fulfil your duty to the kingdom, we'll have to find a new high priestess."

Lyra was about to snap at him when Eve said, "You do not appoint a high priestess. I answer to Adonael, not you, or ultimately, even His Majesty. Nothing you do or say will change reality. Best if you face it now."

Alban reached for his sword. "How dare you speak to a duke in such a tone!"

"That will be quite enough, Alban," Florian said. "If Eve says it can't be done, then we must accept her word as Heaven's representative."

Alban let out a little growl. "Fine. We'll have to rely on the backup plan."

Given what she'd heard so far, Lyra was by no means eager to find out what other stupidity these two had cooked up. Still, she had to know. "And what does your backup plan entail?"

"We'll be recruiting the elf-bloods to fight with the army," Alban said. "Your people have been living off Villipan's charity for far too long. It's time they contributed something."

Lyra's eye twitched and she slowly turned to look at Florian. "What is this buffoon talking about?"

Alban's sword made it halfway out of his sheath before an invisible ethereal hand grabbed him, lifted him off the floor, and slammed him into the far wall.

Lyra never took her eyes off of Florian. "Is it your wish to end the Crown's relationship with me? I agreed to serve your ancestors to provide my people a safe refuge. Take that away and I see no reason to continue to serve."

"You must understand," Florian said, his voice unsteady. "This is an extraordinary circumstance. The kingdom needs more warriors and everyone knows how strong elf-bloods are."

"My people haven't fought anyone in fifteen hundred years. They aren't warriors. And I will not have them turned into warriors. You can have me as an ally or an enemy. Choose."

"You're putting me in a bad position, Lyra," Florian said. "How will it look if the king backs down from one of his servants?"

Lyra narrowed her golden eyes. "How will it look if the king's severed head is placed on top of the castle flagpole? Choose, Florian."

The blood had drained from the boy's face, but she didn't let up her pressure.

At last he said, "Of course we want to maintain good relations with you. The thing is, knights have already been dispatched to conscript your people. Alban said it would be best to get them integrated with the army as quickly as possible."

"I knew you were an idiot," Lyra said. "Richard knew it as well. But even I didn't think you were this stupid. No doubt spending time in the company of Alban Morel has damaged your brain even further. Heaven knows I feel slightly stupider every time I'm forced to speak with him. Since you've decided to breach our agreement, I'll be leaving Villipan City. First I'll deal with your knights, then I'll settle down in our village. If you send more soldiers, I'll bring you their heads then add yours to the pile. I'm done with you and your wars. Have fun when the demon king returns."

Lyra turned and stalked out of the war room. She made it partway down the hall before Eve came running up behind her.

"You can't leave," Eve said. "Who will train the next hero?"

"Should it be necessary, have your successor come find me. Assuming no one troubles us for a century I may reconsider my decision." Lyra stopped and focused on Eve. "Take care of yourself. I don't trust those two fools as far as I can throw a mountain."

Warning given, she marched on. Lyra needed to catch those knights before they could trouble her people.

AUTHOR NOTE

Hello everyone,

I hope you enjoyed Danny's most recent adventure. When next we meet up with him, he'll be on his way to the legendary city of Elfhome. Can't wait to see you there.

If you don't want to miss any of my new releases, deals, general news about the Etherverse, you can signup for my newsletter on my website.

www.jamesewisher.com

Until next time, thanks for reading,

James E. Wisher

ALSO BY JAMES E. WISHER

Summoned to Another Words and Forced to Fight The
Demon King

The Summoned Hero

The Birth of Ronin

The Fate of The Five Kingdoms

The Plague Lands

Elfhome

The Forest of Drakes (Coming March 2026)

The Lord of Black Ice (Coming May 2026)

Unholy War (Coming July 2026)

The Aegis of Merlin:

The Impossible Wizard

The Awakening

The Chimera Jar

The Raven's Shadow

Escape From the Dragon Czar

Wrath of the Dragon Czar

The Four Nations Tournament

Death Incarnate

Atlantis Rising

Rise of the Demon Lords

The Pale Princess

The Divine Key Trilogy

Shadow Magic

For The Greater Good

The Divine Key Awakens

The Portal Wars Saga

The Hidden Tower

The Great Northern War

The Portal Thieves

The Master of Magic

The Chamber of Eternity

The Heart of Alchemy

The Sanguine Scroll

Shadow of The Dragons

The Dragonspire Chronicles

The Black Egg

The Mysterious Coin

The Dragons' Graveyard

The Slave War

The Sunken Tower

The Dragon Empress

The Dragonspire Chronicles Omnibus Vol. 1

The Dragonspire Chronicles Omnibus Vol. 2

The Complete Dragonspire Chronicles Omnibus

Soul Force Saga

Disciples of the Horned One Trilogy:

Darkness Rising

Raging Sea and Trembling Earth

Harvest of Souls

Disciples of the Horned One Omnibus

Chains of the Fallen Arc:

Dreaming in the Dark

On Blackened Wings

Chains of the Fallen Omnibus

The Complete Soul Force Saga Omnibus

Other Fantasy Novels:

The Squire

Death and Honor Omnibus

The Rogue Star Series:

Children of Darkness

Children of the Void

Children of Junk

Rogue Star Omnibus Vol. 1

Children of the Black Ship

Children of The End

ABOUT THE AUTHOR

James E. Wisher is a writer of science fiction and Fantasy novels. He's been writing since high school and reading everything he could get his hands on for as long as he can remember.